TRAZ

Ansell Roberts

BOOKSURGE
WWW.BOOKSURGE.COM

ISBN-10:   1-4196-8697-6
ISBN-13:   978-1-4196-8697-9
Library of Congress Control Number: 2008900602
Publisher: BookSurge Publishing
North Charleston, South Carolina

Visit www.traz.com to order additional copies.

Special Thanks to:

Jean Sider
Paul Burden
Leigh Cofrin
Young Huh

TRAZ

In the Control Room

In a dark, unoccupied room, the illuminated panels stand ready to speak. Their cool, dark, controlled environment will be shaken only by a select few. Only for a time, only for a place . . . an island. Suddenly a rumbling of footsteps and a burst of an open door are heard. The character of the room changes dramatically. Now the lights are on and the Viewers have taken their seats. In an instant, the panels come to life with streaming data and flashing images. Smoke slowly fills the room.

"Oh, I've got a call in," yells a rookie. He presses a button to review the scene.

The screen shows a baseball field where Little Leaguers are playing. When the umpire calls an outside strike on one of his players, the coach shouts to the umpire, "What, you got your head up your ass?" The umpire stops the game and walks over to the coach.

"What did you say?"

"Nothin'."

"That's what I thought you said. If you say anything else, you're outta here!"

The coach's wife is covering her face. Another bad pitch is called a strike and the inning is over. The coach is about to shout something, but the assistant coach covers his mouth. When his team takes the field, the coach urges them to hold their one run lead. Soon there are two outs and no one on base. But his pitcher throws the ball inside and hits the batter, who then takes first base.

The coach is furious and hustles to the mound. He whispers in the pitcher's ear, "If you don't get this next fat ass out, I'm pulling you out of the game." The next pitch is hit and a fly ball sails toward his son, who is playing center field. The boy muffs the catch and it goes past him for a two-run homer. They lose the game.

The coach rushes out to center field, and throws his cap down in front of his son. His wife is still in the bleachers, only this time she's crying. The coach yells, "I don't believe it! I don't believe it! My own son! What have I been teaching you all these years? Here's the damn ball. It goes in the damn glove!" He then slams the ball into the boy's glove, but the boy throws down his glove and runs crying to his mom. The coach is still ranting and raving. As the crowd stares at the coach in disbelief, his wife calls the control room.

After reviewing the scene, the Viewer mutters, "This guy tops the A-hole cake." He enters the offense in the database, and immediately the screen flashes to indicate this is the coach's third and final offense. The Viewer puts down his cigar, and quickly presses the red button, the letter "A" on his keypad. This activates a wireless signal that is sent to the nearest Strikers in the area of the offense. Three sumo-shaped members of the Striker Force quickly emerge onto the field and carry away the coach, who is screaming and yelling. In the stands the mom and son are now hugging each other. His son asks, "Where are they taking Daddy?"

Back in the control room, a man wearing sunglasses turns to the woman Viewer next to him. She is rather thin and has short hair. She is wearing a double-breasted suit and looks as if she could easily fit in on the floor of the New York Stock Exchange. She is staring dispassionately at her screen. The man breaks up her boredom by saying, "Did I tell you what I saw on the screen yesterday?" When she doesn't reply, he continues, "Someone must have alerted us from a luxury hotel in Nob Hill. Well, anyway, my screen showed this beautiful poolside scene—gorgeous cocktail waitresses, crystal blue water, beautiful city skyline—except for a repulsed look on a man's face who was trying to take in its beauty." The woman stares blankly at the man wearing sunglasses, but he continues. "Well, anyway, along comes this whale that fills up my screen—and I'm not talkin' the kind that lives in the ocean. She had cellulite that was dripping like candle wax from her body." The woman's eyebrows form a "V" shape, and she quickly turns toward her screen after making a grunting noise. Unable to take a clue, the man resumes, "Well, anyway, the really sick part was she was wearing a thong. She had her head up, but her ass was draggin' on the ground. Anyway, it was a tough decision on my part, but I let her go. She might have disgusted several people, but it could have been worse.

Yeah, she could have been on a nudie beach." At this, the woman's face turns beet red.

A young man next to him says, "Well, all I know is that I don't have to be sitting in front of this screen to see A-holes."

The man wearing sunglasses asks, "Oh yeah, what do you mean?"

"Well, take for instance yesterday. This was serious stuff, though. I was tuned into the business channel at my girlfriend's place, and they flashed to the Chicago Board of Trade. You know the plane crash of the WMA jet yesterday, with over 100 people killed? Well, as soon as the news broke, several 'opportunists,' shall we say, immediately bought the stock of WMA for $20 a share less. How cold—they even had smiles on their faces in the pit. Before the families of the victims could shed a tear, they descended like vultures."

The female Viewer, although obviously listening to this, continues to stare dispassionately at her screen. The man lifts his sunglasses and asks, "Don't you wish you could have pushed the button on a few of them?"

"Hah! The way they trade tobacco, alcohol, and firearms companies, I would have loved to send the whole Board of Trade to Alcatraz." The young man hesitates a few moments, and then asks, "What do you suppose causes people to be A-holes?"

The man twirls his sunglasses by its straps, and sighs, "I think it's a gene. People are born A-holes."

The young man shakes his head. "That's a convenient excuse, but I think it's when people don't care about anybody but themselves. Let's see how well they'll do when they're in prison with their own kind."

Suddenly, an indiscernible image is displayed on the young man's screen.

"Ah man, we lost the visuals on this one."

A man in the back yells, "Are you gettin' the stats?"

"Yep, his name and social."

"Any prior convictions?"

"None."

"What's his name?"

"Richard Wainwright III."

"The Third? Sounds like an asshole to me."

The young man leans toward the keyboard and laughs.

"That's one for your grand-daddy, one for your daddy, and one for you" as he hits the red "A" button three times.

Another screen reveals a scene of three men, dressed in suits and ties, strolling through the hotel lobby. A raggedy old man, who has been sitting in a corner up to this point, gets up and positions himself in front of the three men. The expression on the raggedy man's face changes to anger.

"You cut funding for the poor . . . homeless people are without shelters," the old man yells.

The man in the middle steps up close to the old man, swiftly knees him in the groin, and as the old man is doubling up, punches him in the face. The old man, with nose bleeding, collapses to the ground.

The man in the middle stands over him and in a Southern accent says, "You're lucky we're not in my hometown in Texas." As the man is saying this, he points to the old man with his index finger extended and thumb up, mocking a gun.

With a grin on his face, he points his index finger upward and blows on the tip of it.

The Secret Service agent on the left says to the man in the middle, "Your tie is a little crooked, Mr. President," as he adjusts the man's tie.

The Viewer, who has been watching in disbelief, exclaims, "Oh, shit." A few seconds later he asks, "Is this out of bounds?"

Another in the control room responds sarcastically, "What do you think?"

"What do I think? Respect for anything with two legs went out with the last administration, that's what I think. I see this kind of crap every time he comes to town. Even after the sweeps, there are always some poor souls that manage to stick around long enough to lose some teeth."

"Hey, hey, hey . . . What's all the chatter?" the supervisor asks sternly.

Silence.

"C'mon, let me punch it just once," the rookie pleads as he replays the presidential scene.

"NO, you can't push the button!" the supervisor replies firmly. "Repeat after me" he says slowly as he stares at the rookie rebel, "T-h-e p-r-e-s-i-d-e-n-t i-s n-o-t a-n a-s-s-h-o-l-e!" The supervisor looks around and notices all of the Viewers in the control room staring at him. He looks down, embarrassed, and walks away from the screen.

The man with the sunglasses leans toward his screen and exclaims, "Oh, here's a classic! I can identify with this."

TRAZ

On his screen, traffic is backed up for a mile on the Golden Gate Bridge. A car is parked across two lanes, and its driver is unloading a tripod and video equipment from his car. The sound of horns is constant. Many cars in view have their windows rolled down, with heads, fists and arms shaking out of the windows. The driver is unfazed as he leisurely strolls to the fence along the side of the bridge. He unpacks his video equipment, and attaches his video camera to his tripod. He then points the camera at Alcatraz Island. The horns are blaring even louder.

The Viewer keeps his focus on the man with the tripod. "Hmmm. That face looks familiar. I think it's the Channel 6 video reporter. What do you think?"

The young man scoots his chair toward the man's screen. "Yep, I could tell by the bright blue blazer. That's him all right. Well, too bad, you know the mayor's policy."

The man responds dejectedly, "Yep," and he hits the "no offense" button.

Back at the traffic scene, the photographer exclaims, "Magnifico!" as he pans Alcatraz. He zooms in on the uppermost part of the island, which shows a large bone-white building. The photographer keys in the word "Alcatraz" on his editing pad, but only part of the word, "traz," appears. Puzzled, he hits the erase button and types in the word "Alcatraz" again. But the first four letters are still missing, and he steps back in bewilderment. He checks his equipment, but everything appears to be functioning. The look of bewilderment turns into astonishment as he says to himself, "Mmmm. 'Traz.' I kind of like it." As he motions with his hand from the bridge to the distant island, "Trazzzz" rolls gently off his tongue. He then adjusts the aperture to decrease the lighting in the lens, and also alters the color. "Trazzzz," he says again while panning from one end of the island to the other. With the press of a button, this video is transmitted over a wireless network to a station in San Francisco.

Seconds later, the same scene flashes on all TVs tuned in to the San Francisco all-news network. At one neighborhood bar, the word "Traz" flashes across a screen portraying a dark, foreboding view of Alcatraz. People who were chatting with each other have now turned their attention toward the large, flat panel display. A newscaster explains, "As everyone knows, Alcatraz will reopen due to the new A-hole law, as we in San Francisco are the first ones to pass this law. Alcatraz is currently two weeks away from being supplied and ready to be inhabited by the first so-called "prisoners," who will be there for a one-year stay. Construction is still under way but on target. Media are still barred from Alcatraz."

Two men are sitting on barstools next to each other. One is unshaven, has tattered clothes, and looks as though he has many hours of sleep to catch up on. The second man is well-dressed in a sport coat and tie. His hair is slicked back, and he is clean-shaven.

The unshaven man turns to the other, "This is a book waiting to be written."

The second man responds, "Hey, it's about time they locked these A-holes up. Look at this." He pulls up the sleeve of his coat and reveals a wristwatch. The push of a button changes the time-keeping display to a monitor, which reveals numerous mug shots accompanied by names, addresses, and a list of offenses for the incoming Alcatraz inhabitants. "All of this information is posted. Here . . ." He points downward. "This is my next door neighbor. I never see the guy; pulls in, pulls out of the drive, like any other schmuck. So I read here . . . are you looking?" The unshaven man struggles to see the screen. "Here I find out that he is world class!" As they review the published offenses, grimaces are mixed with laughter. The images continue to scroll across the small display.

"Recognize anyone?"

"Hey, who's that?" The unshaven man asks as he points to a photo of a pretty young woman. He opens his eyes wider and blinks several times in a struggle to focus.

"Is there room for me?" the clean-shaven man laughs as he nudges the other.

"There's not enough room on the island for all the jerks I know," the unshaven man sneers as his beer mug loudly hits the bar.

"Does that include you?" the other man chuckles. The unshaven man suddenly looks deep in thought. The clean-cut man straightens his tie as he adds, "Hey, my wife has got two strikes against her. I can't wait to get that witch on the last try. The third one should be on looks alone."

"Speaking of jail, I got the warden waiting for me at home." As the unshaven man leaves, he spills some beer trying to put his mug down. He stumbles out, bouncing off a few patrons.

Soon after he leaves, the news sequence continues with a close-up of workers setting up on the island. The commentator adds, "According to information released today by the mayor's office, the island can only hold 200 occupants. There are currently 150 people that have been sentenced. So they're short by 50 jerks." He then cracks a smile as he says excitedly, "We've just completed our call-in survey and here are the top five occupations of people with the highest sphincter factor." A circular target appears on the screen. He continues, "Number five is . . ." and as he says this an icon of an open mouth appears on the outermost ring, "infomercial salespeople." He continues, "Number four is . . ." and now an icon of a taxi appears on the fourth outermost circle as the anchor adds, "downtown taxi drivers." The anchor chuckles, "I can identify with that one. Number three is . . . talk radio jocks. That's a given. Number two is . . ." While he says this an icon of a hand grabbing a bag of money appears on the second innermost target, "lawyers. Now can I have a drum roll? Number one is . . . lawyers, too." He laughs, "I'm surprised the top five weren't all lawyers."

A person in the bar yells at the screen "Hey, he forgot TV preachers. I voted for that four times."

Another voice retorts "Four times? That's $10 a call on their 900 number. You paid $40 for this bullshit survey—you should have called in and said these 900 number operators are A-holes," he says as he laughs.

The first man replies sharply, "How about professional drunks like you?" The two stumble off their stools and start to go toward each other until the bartender interrupts, "If you want to fight, take it outside. I don't mind if you mess up each other's faces, just don't mess up my bar."

Coffee Break

In a high-rise in downtown San Francisco, Tricia gets an early jump on break time.

She searches in a sly, slow, casual manner. The art department was a pit, not literally, but four rows of desks, ten deep. Tricia stays there to answer the phone, and her boss Nan is in her office with the door closed. Tricia casually cruises by the first row of unoccupied desks, starting at the back of the room. Passing up two or three desks on each side of the first aisle, her dark eyes swiftly examine the artists' workstations. She spies a stack of papers on one designer's desk. She stops, and reaching over with both hands, carefully flips through the paperwork, so as not to upset his creative mess. She pulls away, spotting only job-related notes, obviously nothing of interest. It is only three minutes into break time; barely enough time has passed for the employees to squeeze a cup of coffee out of the vending machines. Tricia is in high gear.

Two desks up, toward the front of the room, she makes another stop: Susan's station. A book sitting on a paper catches her eyes. She reaches over to her right. With one hand she slowly shifts the book while her eyes look up and around, searching for a trace of movement. It's safe in the pit, so she lifts the book after seeing some handwriting on a piece of stationery, not office stationery; no, this was personal paper. Her eyes widen while she reads from the top of the page, a perfect find! A goldmine! Tricia says to herself, her mouth almost watering, "Shoulda used e-mail." She cracks a smile and reads:

"You are putting too much pressure on me. You knew this job would demand all of my time during the next few months. I told you it would be exhausting. You knew how stressful it would be and you just keep on it. I can't live like this anymore, thinking about coming home to . . . I have to leave. I just don't love you anymore."

In the meantime, while Tricia is still reading, two writers are about to re-enter the office when they catch a glimpse of her hovering over Susan's desk. The first man pushes his arm in front of his co-worker, stopping him from taking another step.

He whispers, "Look, there she goes again. Damn! Do you believe that? She does it constantly!"

"Why does she do that?"

"I think she's bored and the only excitement is knowing everyone else's business. She doesn't have a life."

"Yeah, you could be right. I know she lives alone, and doesn't have any husband, family, or friends. This must be her only turn-on."

"No friends, really?" the other adds sarcastically.

"She doesn't even have a pet."

"I know she stays at the office very late. I wonder what she's up to after hours."

"Yeah, she always has her door closed, too."

"Look, she's moving toward Nan's office."

The co-worker remarks, "Oh, man, I hope she checks my desk out!"

"Why, you didn't leave that ransom note in the desk drawer again, did you? We need some new material."

"No, no, she's been at this far too long, it's gotta stop. This new one is no 'POP, can of worms, shit in your pants stuff.' This is the real thing, my friend."

They walk back to the break room, while Tricia reports to Nan.

"So not only is her work substandard, and a day behind, but her personal life is also suffering. Look, she's leaving her lover and she's doing it on company time." She hands Nan the stationery. "This girl really needs some time off. Get someone in here who doesn't have all these problems! This is ridiculous. She can't even handle her personal life, let alone her professional one."

Nan's look turns serious as she says, "I check her files daily, they seem to be all right. I thought her work was up to par."

"Well," Tricia stammers, ". . . just barely, but how long will that last with all of this personal trivia going on? Another week and she won't know which end is up. Mark my words, her work is going to suffer." Her voice suddenly takes on a more threatened tone as her head moves closer to Nan's. "I heard that she even tried suicide once. If she pulls something like that again, then where will that leave us? Screwed, that's where!"

"Well, I don't . . ."

"Look, we'll talk about it tonight at Sam's Tap."

"Okay."

"Good. Gotta go; break time's over. See you at seven."

As she leaves Nan's office, the two writers file back in with the rest of the group. The first remarks to the other, "Maybe tomorrow!"

"Tomorrow?"

"Code Red, my friend."

"Co . . ." He looks up, puzzled. "Excuse me?"

"Look, this woman has done this since you and I can remember. This invasion of privacy has gone on long enough. I'm not going to count on Nan to put a stop to it, that's for certain. I'm tired of my desktop being open to public scrutiny. This next time should do it though. Code Red, my friend."

"Explain, please?"

"You know about those dye-packs that are placed in bank bags, don't you? If someone were to open the bag of money, the red dye sprays and covers their hands and what not. Well, I know someone who works at the First National and . . ."

"It's in your drawer?"

"You got it!"

"Oh, baby, blood everywhere."

He chuckles, "Yeah, and one quick call to the Viewer, and it's 'See you around, honey.' The Viewers love it when you add a little 'local color.' We have our fun and she'll have hers, for a year or so."

It's Thursday night at Sam's Tap. The wide screen blares the MVJ channel, and the dance floor moves, literally. There, at the end of the bar, Trish and Nan scan the scene.

Nan comments to Trish, "Look at this. It just occurs to me how ridiculous this really is. Maybe it's something my father said last night. He calls me every now and then." Nan exclaims as a side remark, brushing her short hair back quickly with her hand, "He calls me beautiful, by the way."

"Well, let's see if any one of these young doll boys hits on you tonight, beautiful!" Tricia replies.

"But back to what I was saying. It's ridiculous, this 'club land' scene, I mean . . ." She speaks with a chuckle as her hand motions to the screen. "Listen to this music, look at these people dance. They don't even move, I mean, they just stand in one spot. What do you call that?"

Nan sips her ice-blue seven-seven and shakes her head, eyes fixed on the dance floor.

"They call it 'Zone'," replies Tricia.

"I know that, but . . . I mean, look. They don't even move."

"The dance floor does it for them," adds Tricia, as she looks over at a young male server with no shirt, hoping to catch a wink.

"What does that tell you? And what's all this touchy-feely arm stuff? You have two people facing each other, not even moving; their legs, arms extended as they wave their hands and arms at each other? You know, I've been seeing it for months but it just now strikes me as absurd. My dad likes the good old days, you know, Tricia. He was reminding me of slam dancing."

Tricia chuckles, "That's great . . . and you and your dad stay in touch . . . that's good."

"Yeah, how about you?"

"Me? No."

"Oh, I'm sorry."

"Don't be." Tricia stares ahead, grabs her glass and quickly gulps down the rest of her drink. She immediately motions to the bartender for a refill. She turns toward Nan. "I think we have time for a little story."

"I was like, fourteen years old . . . it was just before Christmas. My mom asked for help with the laundry. 'Trish, get your dad's suits ready for the cleaners.' So I check the pockets and find a receipt from Armand's Jewelry, that nice place downtown. It's a receipt for a three thousand dollar diamond necklace. I thought 'Wow, what a great Christmas surprise for mom! So the two or so weeks before Christmas morning, I'd every now and then smile to myself when mom and I were doing the dishes, or the laundry . . . thinking, 'wait until Christmas morning, are you going to be surprised!'"

"Guess what Nan?" Tricia reaches for the next drink with a tight grip and a quick gulp.

"No necklace. Christmas came and went . . . I never said a word to her. I'm fourteen years old and wondering, 'where is the necklace? Did he forget to give it to her?' I could have asked him but he was out of town the next morning . . . on a business trip. Do you see where this one's going?"

Nan sighs.

"So I started doing some detective work, at least as much as a teenager can do. I looked around the old man's office; his bookshelves, his closet, his drawer, and Bang! In his desk

drawer . . . in our home . . . I find a brown envelope. I open it and slowly pull out a photo. I see a face I've never seen before . . . a blond woman . . . someone I don't recognize. As I pull it out I see that this woman is naked from the waist up! The only thing she is wearing is a fucking diamond necklace! Across her big fat boobs is some handwriting saying 'Thanks for the gift, luv ya baby.' Well, when he slithered back home, I shoved that picture right back in that bastard's face and thanked him for lovin' mom. By New Years Eve, he was gone for good."
Tricia holds her glass up to Nan and smiles.

"The good news is . . . he was gone for good!"
She tilts her head back and laughs.

"Cheers Nan!"
They clank their glasses together in a toast.

Just then they are both distracted by two middle-aged men who approach them from behind.

"Speaking of old bastards . . . ," Nan remarks as she turns around.

"Excuse me," says the first as he struggles to keep his balance. He is aiming his glazed eyes toward Tricia. "I was wondering, can you buy me a drink?"

"Oh, you are smooth," says Nan sarcastically.

"How would you know, honey?" the man replies as he turns away from Nan. He spills his beer; most of it falls on Tricia's lap.

"Crap! You idiot! Look at what you . . ."

The other man interrupts. "Please, he's had a little . . . here, let me . . ." He quickly takes off his shirt and starts to wipe Tricia's lap with it.

"Ah! Get away from me," Tricia screams. "You are disgusting! Help, bartender, get this guy off of me." The two men retreat. Both Nan and Tricia jump off of their barstools as two bouncers escort the men out.

"Oh, you are smooth!" the man comments to his friend.

"Look, Nan, let's discuss Susan tomorrow. We'll do lunch."

They both head toward the exit.

The following morning, Tricia once again makes her rounds during break time. This time, however, she detours to one of the writer's desk. Now there is no one to watch her. Swiftly scanning the desk, she spots nothing of interest, but this does not stop her from a closer and more invasive search. She begins to open the desk drawers. First the top right. Nothing but some work-related manual. Over to the top middle. Nothing of interest. Next over to the bottom left. She looks around, and then opens it. A snapping sound, then a hiss. A look of horror on Tricia's face as she realizes what is occurring. All she sees is red. The red dye-pack planted in the drawer explodes, spraying her hands and legs, and for a little extra punch the spray continues up under her dress. She screams and runs frantically to the ladies room. The blood-curdling scream is heard throughout the floor of the office building.

The writer, sitting in the cafeteria, sipping his coffee, turns to his friend, "Excuse me, I've got a call to make." As he walks away, the other mumbles quietly to himself, "Code Red," and continues to drink his coffee, figuring there is really no rush to this display; the permanent dye will keep her looking "hot" for a very long time. The writer is now in the office room where the dye exploded, and punches a code in his phone. He looks at the trail of red, smiles, and walks away.

Here Comes the Judge

A few months prior, in early January, the mayor of San Francisco was concerned with the red tape involved in sentencing for the A-hole law. He was afraid the newly renovated island would sit idly by while those sentenced would continually appeal their verdicts, and hold up the inhabitation of the island. The city government quickly passed an escape clause for sentencing, tailored exclusively for the A-hole law, with the promise that justice will be swift.

Those sentenced would be taken immediately to isolated holding areas, not jail cells. One of the holding areas is currently occupied by the coach, who only two days ago belittled his son when he dropped a fly ball. Harold the coach is pacing back and forth in his room like a caged animal. The room is painted pink, with pictures of clowns on each wall. They all have different expressions, ranging from happy to sad. There is a twin bed and chair, along with various magazines on a coffee table. He is muttering to himself and gesturing with his hands.

"Fifteen years. Fifteen fucking years!"

Thoughts of his wife preoccupy him. Married for fifteen years, having gone through so much together. He was there by her side when she almost died of pneumonia. He nursed her, he coddled her. How could she turn him in? He played an active role in raising their rambunctious son of nine years. They brought the kid up right, giving him a strict upbringing and a fear of God. How could she turn him in? So he lost his temper on occasion. He never physically beat her. He never touched her! Why did she threaten divorce so often? Why did she turn him in?

"I'll get her back. I'll definitely get her back!"

As a man in black opens the door to the coach's holding area, Harold asks, "Who the hell are you?"

The man sternly says, "Follow me." Harold is escorted from his isolated holding cell and approaches an entranceway to a blackened room. As the guard opens the door, he is greeted by the thick aroma of apple-cherry incense. Smoke circles blue and orange figures as they hover in midair while Harold scans the room decorated with black light images.

"What the hell is this, a head shop?" Harold yells.

All of a sudden a light turns on which reveals a middle-aged woman with teased hair and a halter-top. As the room becomes light, she asks excitedly, "Wanna see my new project?"

As she begins to loosen the knot in her halter, the guard interrupts, "Hold on, Louise, this is government work."

As she tightens her halter up, Harold continues to examine the walls until his eyes catch the farthest corner of the room, where a frozen figure is sitting on a stool. It is a naked man, whose body is stamped with logos. His foot sports the Nike logo, his bulging waist displays a Tire America logo, his forehead shows off the Excedrin symbol, and a glance to the south reveals a Viagra logo. The figure now leans against a painted table. The guard, also noticing the illustrated man, says sarcastically, "Is that on the city's payroll?"

She casually responds, "No, it's a freelance job."

Harold squints as a look of disbelief covers his face. He looks up at the guard as he says, "No fuckin' way she's putting a tattoo on me!"

The guard retorts, "Drop your pants and bend over, asshole!"

"Come on, honey, it won't hurt—it's only a temp."

"Shove those tattoos up your . . ."

"Don't ya wanna see what you're gettin'?"

She opens a portfolio of designs, and turns to a page displaying a large black circle with a red letter "A" in the center. She pushes the book close to his face.

"No fu . . ."

She holds up a syringe with one hand and a tattoo needle with the other.

"Which one will it be, honey?"

As he turns toward the guard, a rifle is aimed at his rear end. As he bends over and mumbles, she exclaims, "Good choice, honey. Hey, before you know it, you'll be wanting another one. It's addictive, you know."

His cheeks tense up, and he unleashes a tirade of profanity while being emblazoned with his new identity. During this process, the illustrated man in the corner of the room grins as he leafs through his magazine. As she swabs Harold's cheek, she exclaims "All done, honey!"

As he hurriedly begins to pull up his pants, he meets resistance as she grabs his belt loop. She forcibly turns his head around to face the mirror on the back wall. "Don't ya wanna see it?"

"NNOOOOO!" he screams as he catches a glimpse of the emblem on his buttocks: a blood red "A" inside of a black circle on his right cheek. As he tightens up, the circle becomes an ellipse. Instinctively he rubs his hand back and forth over the tattoo, but to no avail, as it is one with his body. He wrings his hands in frustration.

"Another masterpiece! Now you can pull up your . . ." the artist excitedly exclaims with a smile.

Before she can finish, the guard grabs Harold's arm and forcibly escorts him to court.

As they pass through a narrow hallway, a woman dressed in blue is passing in the other direction. She is walking very fast with her nose up in an air of superiority, avoiding eye contact. Harold mumbles to himself, "Blue Nazi fast-stepper." He turns to the guard immediately before entering the courtroom and yells, "What kind of a fuckin' law is this? A few years ago, our country was a pussy when it came to punishing criminals, even murderers got off."

"Let's go."

"Listen, I did nothing and now I might end up on Alcatraz. That's more punishment than we used to . . ."

"Let's go!" The man's inflection sharpens as he tightens the grip on Harold's arm, and leads him into the room.

As the door swings open, darkness seeps out. Suddenly a spotlight shines into Harold's face, and he tries to deflect it with his forearm and a wince of an eye. He is led a few feet to his right, where the spotlight now shines on a small wooden chair.

"What da?"

"Just sit down!" the guard barks.

As Harold squeezes uncomfortably into the chair, he glances around the darkness. The glare of the spotlight is now removed. Instead, a blue glow highlights a large desk that stands twenty feet in front of him, and a dozen feet above Harold's chair. He cranes his neck to peer up, but all he can discern is a pair of hands clasped above the desk.

He is now involuntarily trembling, caught in an uncomfortable mix of fear and anger. Harold clears his throat, and talks sternly at the shadow behind the pair of hands. "Judge, I'm not prepared to meet in court without a lawyer."

"You've been accused of violating the A-hole law."

"Accused? You already convicted me. You turned my ass into a pincushion!"

The judge continues, "Under the statutes of the law, no lawyer or jury is required. We will replay your three offenses, after which time you may comment on any of them."

A large screen lights up to the right of the judge. The screen replays Harold bitching at a waitress in a restaurant because he was not seated at a table with the scenic view. His outburst continues as his coffee is not hot enough to his standards, and he purposely spills it on the floor. The waitress is in tears as she bends down to wipe the carpet with a rag.

With a look of disgust, Harold shakes his head.

A second scene is replayed from the Monterey Bay Aquarium. "Look at that Great White, Donny!" Harold exclaims in amazement. His son screams into the glass to capture the shark's attention, but the shark quickly swims past. As Harold turns to scold his son, Donny takes a wad of gum out of his mouth and sticks it onto the aquarium glass. Harold is now stone-faced and beet red. As he is about to scold him again, Donny screams and attempts to run away. Harold quickly catches him and tightly squeezes his son's hand, pulling him up a spiral staircase. At the top of the stairs, Harold glances around as his eyes land on a door marked "Employees Only." He quickly opens the door, which leads to the top of the aquarium. "Where are we going Daddy?" But there is no response as he pulls his son's arm toward the edge of the aquarium. He then hoists his son over his head, upside down. His son is now dangling over the tank where the Great White resides. His son is screaming with hands waving.

"What the shit, that wasn't even in San Francisco." Harold begins to raise his voice. "You call these offenses? You're wasting your time and my time. Why don't you get the real assholes up here? Sure, I might have acted like a jerk sometimes, but that's because I have to deal with jerks every day. I just give them a taste of their own medicine. Just remember, if you sentence me, you'll end up being the real asshole."

His third offense is replayed, but Harold's attention has moved from the screen to the judge.

"I'm gonna lose my fuckin' job for this stuff? Who's gonna feed my family?"

There is no reply from the judge. As the last offensive scene finishes, the judge commands, "By order of the court, you are found guilty."

Upon hearing this, Harold grunts and grits his teeth.

"You are sentenced to one year on Alcatraz." At this, the gavel is slammed down hard.

"Next."

The Mayor

On Alcatraz the construction workers are behind schedule and cutting corners whenever and wherever possible. The construction foreman says to the workers, "Hey, we're low on studs. Just space 'em twice as far apart. And we're running short on time—forget putting the insulation in. And . . ." A worker cuts him off, asking, "Isn't that against code?"

The foreman replies angrily, "We get paid by the job, and we have to finish in two weeks." He hesitates a few seconds and continues, "Remember who'll be living here."

With this mandate, the workers' habits get sloppier. In the remaining condos, the hot and cold-water taps are reversed and the drywall is primed but not painted. At the end of the week the foreman gives the Mayor of San Francisco a call informing him, "We'll be finishing as planned. Everything looks in tip-top shape."

The mayor is very happy to hear this, and exclaims, "Excellent. I had no doubts." The mayor then turns to his advisor and says, "We're ready to send the boats there. Is everything coordinated on our end?"

The advisor nods.

The mayor adds, "Good. You know, very little in the last few years has given me as much pleasure as passing this law. It's a personal favorite of mine."

The advisor counters, "And you know how I feel. There are so many A-holes out there; Alcatraz is not a practical solution. We would have to put prisons in everyone's backyard."

The mayor furrows his brow and exclaims, "Look, we're not trying to lock up the whole world, we're just setting an example. Remember my image for re-election—'tough on crime.' If it works here, which I know it will, the rest of the cities across the country will adopt this law."

The advisor counters, "This is not something to experiment with."

The mayor bolts up and says in a loud voice, "Of course not, it's beyond that now—it's the law. How many times have you said to yourself, 'This guy is a real asshole. The law isn't going to do anything with him—I wish I could just blow him away.'"

"You said it right—'How many times?' That's the point. It happens too often. It's an impractical law. Why do you think people want to escape from things? They stare at the TV for hours, or get away from everything and crack open a few beers in the middle of a lake and say they're fishing. It's because they want to escape from A-holes. This is still the best way . . ."

The mayor interrupts, "The point is we are still not taking care of the problem!"

He then switches his train of thought to Alcatraz' structure and says, "Hey, come over here." The advisor hesitatingly walks toward the desk. The mayor says enthusiastically, "I've been studying the blueprints for this place. Look at this! Where once you had iron bars, now there's drywall and paneling. Instead of having to shit in a corner, they each have their own private bathrooms. Geez, this is an asshole resort. They're even riding a tour boat to get to the island. Plus they even get to bring on two pieces of luggage."

The mayor gets up from his chair and looks out the window of his high-rise office building. As he stares out the window, he says sarcastically, "Yeah, I'm thinking of taking my wife there for our second honeymoon." Between puffs, he rolls his cigar between his fingers and stares at it. He then laughs as he says, "On second thought, maybe I'll leave her there. But seriously, the only thing this place doesn't have is a golf course."

The mayor's campaign manager adds, "Maybe we could make this a new tourist attraction. People could view all the A-holes together in an everyday life setting. We could have boats circle the island. Maybe we could get the marketing committee to make striped T-shirts for the jerks on the island."

The mayor jumps up and adds, "How about souvenirs—maybe we could sell Alcatraz in a bottle—shake it up and it snows red A's on Alcatraz."

The campaign manager adds, "We need to get some inside pictures of you inspecting the island."

Mayor laughs, "I wouldn't want to get within 100 yards of these losers—they're not locked up remember."

The advisor says, "It's funny now, but . . ."

The mayor interrupts again, "As someone once said—'it's a done deal.'"

Back at Alcatraz, one of the workers shouts, "What? The shitter's boiling over!"

"Looks like we have to come back tomorrow to get the plumbing straight," another worker sighs.

"One shitter? No way," the first worker snaps back. "I tee off tomorrow at 7:00 AM."

The Trip

With construction complete, the prisoners are rounded up from their holding cells and transported by several rusted-out, psychedelic relic VW buses to Pier 33. Paisley decals decorate the side panels. On the bus that Harold is on, the nailed-on stereo speakers blare, "If you're goin' to San Francisco, be sure to wear flowers in your hair."

Someone in the back yells, "Hey, I smell reefer!" The bus driver, who resembles Granny Clampit, has one hand on the wheel and the other on a roach clip.

Harold yells, "I'm in a fuckin' time warp! Hey guard, get me the hell out of here!"

As the driver inhales deeply, she turns around and looks toward the guard, who's passed out. She passes the clip to a passenger behind her saying, "Give this to that honey; he needs to relax."

Suddenly spotting a police car in her rear view mirror, she breaks away from the tail end of the caravan of buses.

"Oh, shit, it's the heat!" She continues, "Swallow that joint, honey!"

As a passenger yells, "The cherries are on!" she floors it. The sirens are now blaring, as she swerves in and out of traffic. A passenger sticks his head out the window and his finger down his throat, forcing himself to throw up. The vomit hits the windshield of the police car, causing it to swerve from lane to lane. A woman in the back of the bus writes with her lipstick on the window, "Help! We're kidnapped in the '60s."

Granny takes the bus down an extremely steep hill, yelling, "Hang on! Turbulence!"

The passengers bounce up and down, some bumping their heads on the ceiling of the bus.

"Whoa, bitch!" one of them yells. "This isn't a fuckin' rodeo!"

"Hey, let's get out of San Fran."

Others join in yelling, "Yeah, turn around!"

Crossing an intersection, she just misses hitting a dozen people and runs over a sawhorse. Now hundreds of people are crossing that intersection, and the police are halted in their pursuit. The people in back of the bus look back at the marchers, as one of them inquires, "Who are those freaks?"

A woman on the bus states, "It's the 2nd Annual Straight-Rights Parade. My boyfriend and I marched in it last year."

After a few turns, granny abruptly stops the bus. "All out!"

The baggy-eyed guard next to her now wakes up and echoes, "All out!" But none budge. The guard spins his gun as if it's a Roy Roger's pearl-handled six-shooter. Now they all file out. Some passengers are pale. Under heavy guard, they now join the end of the line that is filing onto the cheerfully painted boat, the Harbor Empress, which is poised to leave

Pier 33. The fog is quite thick, and the sounds of the footsteps on the prisoners' pier become louder as the prisoners grow silent. As the last of the prisoners board, the guards follow suit, and verbally signal to the captain to begin the journey. The boat slowly and quietly starts from the pier. There is one more sound, however, emerging from the pier—rushing footsteps in the distance, silence, and then a splash. To the prisoners it may have been a pebble tossed across the waves. But to the two panting police officers on the pier, the sound of that silhouette diving into the bay may as well have been clanging cymbals. This is the second time in a week he's gone—out of sight.

Unbeknownst to the officers, this shadow of a man has latched onto a decorative ornament on the back of the Harbor Empress. He wonders exactly where he's going, how long it will take to get there, and if he should have latched onto the boat at all. He feels the boat accelerating and looks back as it moves farther from the dock. His wet hands struggle for a better grip as he feels the ornament loosening. Should he let go now? It's almost too late, as he's several hundred feet from shore.

Should he jump? Is it still too late to swim back?

He hangs on, but as the boat accelerates, it becomes increasingly difficult. How long, he thinks. How long . . .

"Might as well enjoy the ride; the island's not too far from here," a voice whispers on the upper deck. There is no response from fellow passengers. Of course, all the prisoners know Alcatraz is only a mile from shore. This silence is very disconcerting to some of the people, and the uneasiness becomes more apparent on their faces. The only sound is sniffling as tears roll down a prisoner's cheeks.

As they approach the island, the silence remains. Time has slowed down. Most of the future islanders' eyes are now fixed on the landmass ahead. Their uneasiness grows.

The hard edges of the cliffs are repeated in the structure that sits atop the island. No gentle slopes into the water— all rugged rock. The trees and grass do nothing to soften the effect. The grass seems isolated in its struggle for color. The trees reach out in an attempt to escape.

Suddenly, the water and sky blend into one. The island appears to be floating in its own universe, apart from any connection to the real world. Like Alice in Wonderland going through the looking glass, they would soon disappear into another existence. As they get closer, all that is imprisoned by the nether world seems to grow larger, even more threatening, adding a new urgency to the fears of the newcomers. Some decrepit buildings first make their appearance: one by the lighthouse and a few alongside the shore. Two large buildings are in panoramic view. The four-story building near the dock looks like an old army barracks, and another building atop the hill resembles a warehouse. Which building is their new home?

The boat slows down as it nears the dock. Barely hanging on, the figure breathes a sigh of relief as his eyes look up in thanks. Now he can see the dock. But which island? Treasure Island? Angel Island? As the boat nudges the dock, it's just enough to knock him and the wooden mermaid into the water. As his body is submerged in the water, he starts to realize how cold the water actually is. He swims to the ladder on the side of the pier and waits. Dripping, he overhears a conversation above.

"This was a big tourist attraction? You'd have to be nuts!"

The other person sighs, "So was Pearl Harbor."

A voice from behind says angrily, "Hey, I saw both of them—what about it?"

The cold figure then hunches forward, and says to himself, "Oh, no!" He is still afraid of being seen, so climbs onto a diagonal log under the dock, his legs still dangling in the water.

The prisoners hesitatingly exit the ferry onto the pier. As they step off the boat, they notice the weather-beaten cell house perched on the upper level above the rocks.

One of the new islanders wonders aloud, "Why me? I'm not a hardened criminal. I'm not living in there!"

On the edge of the dock stands a two-way communication screen, its high-tech design and bright colors in contrast to the barren dock it towers above. When the last of the new islanders is on the dock, the fifty-foot wide screen becomes animated with the face of the mayor. A booming voice is projected toward the prisoners, "Welcome A-h . . ." and the mayor's head quickly turns to the left. "OK, OK, ahem . . . islanders. This is John Kravity, Mayor of San Francisco. Enclosed in the two large boxes to the north end of the pier are packets of information, indicating everything you need to know from A to Z in order to live comfortably on this island. The packet tells you what work details you will need and where everything, including your luxurious supplies and penthouses, is located."

After a pause, the mayor continues, "Oh, by the way, one

more thing." He now raises his voice. "Drop your pants. That's right. Drop your pants and bend over! The boys with the steel want to see that big red 'A'." In shock, the islanders' jaws drop. The cocking of firearms backs up the mayor's request. The islanders turn around to what looks like a firing squad.

The mayor continues, "What we have here is a failure to communicate. Now we have to account for all you folks, and the guards are getting a little impatient, if you know what I mean."

At this latest request, a line of plump flesh and cellulite suddenly decorates the dock. One guard comments, "What is this, a billiard room?"

The guards laugh, and another joins in, "Let's have an ugly ass contest—it'll be a hundred-way tie."

Another responds, "Hey, look what's on this one's cheek— 'Kiss me, I'm Polish.'"

A Voice of Discontent then yells, "Hey, fat ass, I got something for your !#@$$!! wife!" He then turns around, exposing himself to the mayor. But before he could finish this sentence, the screen turns blank. A rifle butt strikes the cheek of the Voice of Discontent, and he drops to the dock floor.

As the guards leave, the islanders quickly cover their cheeks. Many are shouting profanities. As the figure under the dock sees the boat leave, he pulls himself onto the dock and runs to hide from the rest of the group.

Their new home's imposing look has taken their thoughts hostage. They first notice the old guard tower. "Will there be a guard stationed up there?"

A voice in the crowd yells, "Don't you know how to read?

The Chronicle said no guards will be on the island. They're not worried about us leaving, they just don't want anyone else here." He then points up at a post, which houses a light and camera facing the bay. At the edges of the island, there are five surveillance cameras pointing out toward the water. Many uncomfortable, puzzled looks appear in the crowd.

Some notice a decrepit brick building. "Is that our prison?" Others turn around, and at the sight of this a thin, frail man lets out a sigh and faints. He collapses on the dock, but no one pays any attention.

A few rip open the boxes, and a free-for-all ensues. As a result of much pushing and shoving, an older woman lands on her keester. Some packets are torn; others are tossed on the dock. A few people with packets hurl them into the bay. The mayhem subsides when no packets remain in the box. Some moaning and groaning ensues, as a few people are still searching for packets. In the distance, the boat whistles as it leaves the dock, but it goes unnoticed.

The islanders feverishly open up their packages, with the exception of the few who have already left the dock to wander around their new habitat, and a few who are observing the melee. The first item in their packet is a full-color map and brochure, oddly depicting the mayor to the left of Alcatraz and a black-and-white vignette of Al Capone to the right.

Somebody says, "What is this, a tour or a sentence?"

A voice in the crowd remarks, "What are all these red 'Xs' marked on this map?"

Another voice jumps in. "Hey, knucklehead, read what it says in the footnotes. 'These 'Xs' are unmaintained buildings which one should not go near.'"

A deep voice grumbles, "They're on everything, except two buildings."

A high-pitched voice shrieks, "We're on a condemned island!"

On the next sheet there is a table displaying information on work details: where each task is to be done, and the location of each piece of equipment to carry out the work detail. It also lists the locations of the instructions needed to operate the facilities on the island. At the bottom of the task sheet in fine print it says:

1. You are a self-sufficient community. A scan of everyone's background finds you have all the skills and expertise required to execute all needed tasks on this island.

2. The exceptions to the above are rehabilitation and health care. A professional counselor, Dr. Rench, will provide organized therapy sessions in addition to private counseling. Therapy sessions are mandatory.

3. The supplies you have will last approximately one month. After that time you will be responsible for ordering your supplies based upon your reasonable needs.

The Voice of Discontent yells, "#$%!! Because we're here for only a year, they're not giving us jack, not even a &%$!! warden. Son-of-a-#!$!!."

Voices from the crowd are shouting.

"How are we going to divide up the work?"

"Who's gonna be in charge on this island?"

Mutterings are heard as a tiny man yells, "I've had positions leading committees, I'll be happy to be a leader for this island."

Another states, "I used to be a mayor for our town. I'll run for leader of this island."

But an elderly man counters, "I don't want any crooked politicians being my leader on this island."

Another hollers, "Me neither. We don't need a King A-hole."

One woman steps in the middle and says, "If we have conflicts, let's do a majority vote. Then we don't need a leader. Who's in favor of majority rule for decisions made on this island?"

More shouting from the crowd.

A prisoner cries out as he leaves the dock, "Fuck the majority vote. Everyone's on their own."

"Nobody's gonna tell me what the hell I can do!" Another leaves the dock.

"Hey, don't include me in your asshole vote."

With all of this dissention, only a few raise their hands.

But the woman in the middle, ignoring the dissention, continues, "OK. Now let's divvy up the work. There are enough jobs for everyone listed in this packet. I'll post this list in the dining hall—wherever that is—and we'll take volunteers, first come first served. The jobs that are left over that nobody wants—well, we'll draw straws for those jobs from the people who don't volunteer."

A woman with heavy make-up scans the jobs listed in the packet and exclaims, "Hey, they don't list beauticians in here—I'm a beautician."

A bald man turns to an overweight fellow standing beside him, "Hey, tiny, if you can suck that gut in a few yards, you could be our personal trainer."

Another barks, "Hey, how about astrologists?"

The bald man tells both the beautician and the astrologist, "You better volunteer for somethin', otherwise you'll be cleaning windows and toilets."

"Toilets—arghh?" the beautician mutters as if she just sucked on a lemon.

The Voice of Discontent yells, "I'm not signing up for anything, I shouldn't even #$%!! be here!"

A man in overalls yells, "They took away my real job, and I'm gonna work in this hell-hole for free? Are you nuts?"

The islanders gradually disperse. Some turn their attention to the four-story building immediately in front of them, a short distance from the dock. This white-painted brick building has yellowed, with chipped paint revealing the brick, and green patches indicating that wildlife has begun to take over. A sign attached to this building displays the bold type-faced headline: "United States Penitentiary." This sign appears to be surrounded by the much larger handwritten phrases "Indians Welcome" and "Indian Land," painted in blood red.

One voice in the crowd yells, "Get me outta here. The Indians can have their damn land back!" Curiosity begins to eat through the crowd as a few of the islanders cautiously head toward this stern building.

Before they enter the building, a scared voice echoes, "Is this one of the condemned ones?"

New Land

"Where's the light switch?"

"Right here."

After a click the room is now dimly lit, displaying many chairs and a projection screen hanging on a wall.

"This doesn't look like the pen."

"Let's see what's upstairs."

A voice booms over a rumble of footsteps, "I can't see where I'm goin'. Where's the stair lights?"

"Owww. Son-of-a-bitch!"

"Who's bumpin' into me?"

A flip of a switch is heard but still no lights. The darkness halts them halfway up the stairs.

As they scurry back down, the first-floor lights are suddenly turned off and they hear the sound of a door slam. A horrible noise is now heard: Thud-thud-thud.

"Ow, damnit! Wait till I get the guy who turned off the fuckin' lights!"

As they search for the door, a beam of light suddenly illuminates a projection screen. Everyone turns in surprise toward the screen, as they see an old film clip of Alcatraz with a stern voice saying: "America's Devil's Island, the home of the most notorious criminals." Suddenly a light shines through a crack in the door, and all inside quickly exit the old prison theater.

Past the old barracks, through the dark tunnel of what was once the guardhouse, the islanders scurry. The geraniums are dancing in full bloom near the guardhouse, teasing the visitors with an array of lavender, bright red, magenta, white, and pink. If any eyes were to gaze past the officers' club ruins, they would see a green coastal prairie, which sports a Midwestern look. But there is no need to look past the ruins, as the road to their new home winds in the opposite direction.

On the road ahead, past the "condemned" electric repair shop, stands a weather-beaten chapel, also marked "Condemned" on the islanders' map. This small, Spanish-style structure is up the road past the guardhouse. Pale white and peeling paint everywhere, it looks as if it has not seen a visitor in decades. Yet in front of its stairs sits one beaten piece of luggage. The right double door is open, but inside is darkness. Through the open frame that once held a window, the movement of a figure draped in white can barely be seen.

Further down the long, steep road to the right is a brick retaining wall, where an older man has just stopped to put down his luggage. He flexes his hand to get feeling back in it. As he pats his brow with a handkerchief, he lifts his panting, sweating head as it swings to the right. In the corner of his eye, he catches a glimpse of a familiar scene. After doing a double take, his face changes from a pale color to a warm glow of astonishment. He slowly walks toward the wall, as if approaching an altar. He stops an arm's length from the wall, and kneels down. With his hand shaking, he slowly moves it toward the wall. He gently caresses a leaf between his two fingers, and places his nose next to the leaf. As he inhales, the lush, green ivy spreading across this brick wall brings back golden memories to him. As he places his Cubs hat over his chest, a tear rolls down his cheek. He mumbles to himself, "Friendly Confines."

The road zags in the opposite direction as it moves up another level on the island. Up this hill to the right are an Australian tea tree and a California Fern, reaching out through a variety of weeds. The road meets another juncture, and continues on to a rusty water tower. A garden of purple irises, orange watsonias, and yellow poppies is ready to greet visitors before reaching the water tower, but no one takes notice, for this is not the path to the islanders' new home. At this juncture, Harold looks on his map and sharply turns to his left to continue another uphill climb. As he glances upward, an enormous building shouts at him. He can see the top two stories of this pale, eroding structure, with its grey matrix of windows, its sharp contour, stern Federalist columns, and chipped and peeling body. His new home. At the thought of this, his stomach does a somersault. He tries to press up the hill, but his arms feel weaker and his luggage slips from his hands.

Further along this path, the purple and red firecrackers and white callas reach out to the gulls and herons. At the end of the path is the burned-out warden's house, an outer shell housing the remnants of an ivy-covered fireplace. Red valerian is growing inside the battered structure, and a variety of roses decorate the outside perimeter. As one continues on the path and turns to the right, both the cell house entrance and enormous lighthouse can be seen. The foreboding, cement grey structure known as the lighthouse perfectly complements the islanders' new home. Tricia approaches the base of the lighthouse, looking toward the top of the towering structure as if ready to open a Christmas present. She approaches the door of the tower, and turns the handle but it does not open. Her expression is one of concern as she pulls on the handle, but to no avail. She picks up her luggage, takes a few steps away from the tower, and then looks back. "I'll be back," she murmurs to herself as she struts to her new home.

Although some started out in a rush, each islander slows down or stops as he or she is approaching the entrance to the old cell house. The large entrance appears to be a black hole, ready to change the status of each one who enters from "visitor" to "prisoner." For some, this is where reality suddenly crashes down. The misleading words "Administration Building" are emblazoned across the top of the entrance. Above this is a large plaque of an eagle whose claws are holding a shield draped in the U.S. flag. This plaque provides the only color for their new home. Past the entrance is a dark alcove, and inside this alcove is a small door, which beckons the islanders into another world.

Some of the islanders are already past this door. They are wandering through the maze of rooms near the entrance, which were at one time the warden's office, the armory, the control room, and the visitation room of the old cell house.

Once past these rooms, they capture their first glimpse of the interior of their new home. The perimeter of the building has not changed since it was a U.S. penitentiary, with its windows to the outside still dressed in thick, iron bars. Along each hallway are condo units, with a staircase leading to an upper level with more of the same. One thin coat of beige paint has been hastily applied to these hallway walls, with drywall showing through in various places that the painters missed. The doors to these units have also been painted over with a coat of beige, and each has a plain knob with no key entry.

As the islanders stake claims to their new homes, many immediately attempt to lock their doors. But there are no locks. This induces panic in some, as loud screams are heard down the hallways. Others construct their own locks by tying clothes from the door handle to fixed parts in the room. Others position a chair or dresser in their room up against the door handle. But there is one woman, when after discovering no locks, has a devious smile on her face.

The condos down aisles "B" and "C" have no view of the outside, and at first remain empty. The condos in the "D" aisle of the old cell house have a view of the bay, and are the first to be populated. The condos in "A" aisle face the San Francisco-Oakland Bridge, and are now filling up on both levels. Any view of the civilized world is better than none and that especially holds true for these prisoners. Even the filthy portals with their checkerboard pattern created by the steel bars protecting them become priceless.

"I was here first!"

"No, you weren't. My luggage was right outside the condo

before you stepped foot here!"

As a wrestling match between the two new islanders ensues, a voice yells, "Girls, girls, break it up!"

"How dare you call me a girl, I'm a woman!" retorts one.

"And how dare you call me a girl, I'm a man!" shouts the other.

"Then go ahead, just let me get through," responds the peacemaker.

There is much traffic up and down the spiral staircase near the "A" aisle, as the mad scramble continues. A little while later, all the condos with an outside view are taken, and a few try bartering for these rooms.

"If you'll switch condos with me, I'll get you a year's worth of free salami when we get off here—I've got my own butcher shop."

"I'll give you seven boxes of Trojans; they're in my briefcase—please open up!"

"My daughter lives in San Fran; please let me wave to her each night. I'm an old lady with not much longer to live!"

Despite these pleas, the doors to these coveted condos remain "shut." The rest of the islanders are stuck down aisles "B" and "C." One islander even walks down the halls sarcastically spewing, "I'm livin' down Broadway and close to Times Square."

One figure, shivering horribly and dripping wet, is running frantically down the hallway. His teeth are chattering like a wind-up dime store mouthpiece. He sees no open doors, so knocks on a random door.

"Taken!" a petite voice counters.

"I just need some dry clothes."

"Taken!"

After a few moments, he shakes his head and continues on, knocking on a door a few units down the hall.

"Get another room, loser," booms a baritone voice from within the unit.

He repeats the process another time. After knocking on the door, a loud belch is returned. He yells, "Have mercy! I need some dry clothes."

Silence.

As he turns away, he notices a ray of light in the hallway. Running toward it, he realizes it's coming from an open door. Can it be? An unoccupied unit? The last unit in the hallway? As he approaches the doorway, his eyes dart around. His heart skips a beat. No one.

His eyes quickly zero in on a single bed in the center of the room, with a bed sheet half-strewn across it. He strips his dripping clothes off, and leaps onto the bed, wrapping himself inside the bed sheet like soft serve into a cone. His teeth are still chattering, but his eyes are fixed on the ceiling. One incandescent light bulb is hanging from a cord. Drywall covers the rest of the ceiling, with fault lines marking where the pieces of drywall collide. No taping, no painting, no finishing.

He then sits up, and gazes around the room. The walls are in the same shape as the ceiling. To the left of the bed is a nightstand, but there is no chair or night-light. In the corner of the room is a dark doorway, and he wonders where it leads. He slowly lifts himself off the bed. As he takes a few steps, he notices a difference in the surface beneath him. Part of the room is tiled, but the rest of the room is a cement floor, which chills his feet. This jigsaw pattern of the tile appears to have no rhyme or reason. He notices something scrawled on the cement below his feet, and bends down for a closer look. It looks like roman numerals are etched in the cement. Puzzled, he gets up and continues toward the dark passage.

He can only see darkness at first. He slowly attempts to enter this space, possibly another room, when his hand bumps against an object. He steps back and again reaches into the entrance. He comes into contact with the object, and rolls his hand around it. His hand feels the length of the object, up and down. His other hand does the same. He grasps both of his hands around the bars, which block his entrance into the other space. His expression sinks as he feels for the first time the history of his new home, a home where people were imprisoned behind these bars.

His eyes adjust to the darkness beyond, and he glances toward the right corner of this space. He now moves toward his right, and sees his reflection in this object, but it is a fragmented reflection. He finds himself staring at a broken mirror behind the bars. He barely recognizes the pale, desperate figure he's looking at. The only highlight is the reflection of his golden tooth, which is the only sparkle in the room.

To the other islanders, this dark space was a finished bathroom. To this islander, it was a reminder of this island's past.

Settling In

After a few hours the new islanders settle in. Many gather in what is marked on their maps as the dining hall, which is the room adjacent to the main block of condos. There is a crowd gathered around the sign-up sheet for tasks.

"Hey, who crossed my name off as barber and put me down cleaning toilets?"

"Give me that pen!"

"How many librarians do they need? I'll put my name next to these three anyway."

"Hey, they'll need somebody to deliver the mail. I'll just add a line at the bottom with my name."

"You can't do that. OK then, I'll add a line 'Gambling Instructor' with my name next to it."

"This sign-up sheet looks like a bomb hit it—I'll make a new one."

"No, give it to me!"

A struggle then ensues, with the list being ripped in half.

"Let's make a new one. I'll pass it around. The last one to get it tapes it to the door."

"If nose one is from Cajun countra, I go in the kitch and stot doin' ma thing."

The Louisiana chef had demanded the kitchen, mostly because of his size. But the first day a ruckus occurred in the kitchen, with pots and pans being thrown about. The big figure lurched out, screaming, "No fud! No fud!" The news spread like wildfire.

Indeed, that first day there was no food, as the supplies did not arrive. The supplies, including food, are to arrive at the dock once a month. At least that's what the package states.

Suddenly, Edvard Munch's *The Scream* comes to life, "We'll starve if we have to wait a whole month for food!"

"Get your silly ass by the dock and round us up once they arrive," a voice adds with authority.

"Fuck you! You wait by the dock!"

Without any food, the islanders angrily leave the dining hall and retire to their condos. One of them bolts out of his room and yells to others gathered in the condo hallway, "Hey, where's room service? How can I call room service? Does anybody have a phone?" The others shake their heads in disbelief as he continues, "My Lord, it's been a day without TV."

One of the others says sarcastically, "Yeah, you'd think they just stuck us here to punish us or somethin'."

The first yells back, "Even in real jails, the prisoners get cable TV." As they are walking away the man continues, "I asked for a condo overlooking the Golden Gate Bridge, but some selfish people took those."

There is not much social interaction in the hallways, and the night is very quiet.

This evening a priest approaches the chapel, which he has been cleaning since his arrival. He notices a small light in the window. As he squints his eyes, he notices the door is ajar. He slowly walks down the inclined path and climbs the weathered stairs to the Chapel. He hesitates at the front door and looks through the crack. He sees the silhouette of a figure sitting with his back toward the door, facing an empty void that could have once been the altar of the modest church. A single candle is burning on the side table. As the priest slowly opens the door, he gets a better view of the figure. It's a young, bald man with a slight build. The priest also begins to hear the whisper of a song.

". . . God is bigger than the boogie man,
God is bigger than the boogie man,
and He'll take care of me . . ."

The bald man is clasping his hands, with his head bowed down in deep thought. He is preoccupied with a stream of thoughts from when he was a little boy, staying at St. Jude Children's Hospital.

A little boy, in the darkness of a building so strange to him. All the people he didn't know . . .

All he could do was miss his mom. She left him all alone, but she couldn't help it; that's what they told him. He was told by these new people that it was okay to cry. And he did. The tears made him feel better. Any little boy who couldn't see his mom would cry too.

He lay down on this new bed. It wasn't as soft as his. He

turned his head and stared at the small light across the room. It was left on for him. He was so scared. In a small crackly voice, he began to sing just like his mom said to do whenever he was scared.

She would sing with him; she smiled a lot when they did.

". . . God is bigger than the boogie man,
God is bigger than the boogie man,
and He'll take care of me . . ."

It was light and the little boy woke up to noise, to happy noise, voices of kids laughing. He sat up. He looked across the room. A girl even bigger than him jumped up and down on her bed with all of her might. She made big fists and jumped up and down until she almost touched the ceiling! She laughed as she jumped, "I'm going home! I'm going home!" All the rest of the boys and girls woke up now. Some laughed. Some jumped on their beds, too. Some couldn't; they were too tired.

The little boy smiled as he shouted, "I'm going home!" When he stopped, he wished it would be him.

But it would take a while; he would have to be bald first. Just like that girl.

"God is bigger than the boogie man . . ."

"Hey skinhead! You with the NBA or the swim team? With a body like that?

The boy just stared as he bit his lip in anger. He stood strong and still, holding his schoolbooks. "Don't you know?" another antagonizing voice added, "he does it for his friends;

he looks like Uncle Fester 'cause of his friends."

"I didn't think he had any friends. Oh! That's right. His cute little friends are sick."

"Yeah, but can they play basketball? Ha ha ha ha!"

"Tony!"

The boy turned as a classmate called to him.

"Don't let them get to you."

She stood close to him, "Let's go."

She tugged.

He stood there like a rock as his stare pierced the back of each of them. The boy let the others get 20 feet down the school hall until they just started down the stairway—he dropped his books, grabbed the back of his head with his hands, elbows out, and started running down the hall. As he approached within 5 feet of the others, he fell to the floor in a high-speed somersault, flying into the gang of boys. A rumble, screams and a crash. The gang of rudes dropped to the floor like bowling pins.

The bald man turns his head and stares at the small light across the room. He gently runs his hand over the top of his smooth head, his symbol of defiance.

"You want a donation for these kids. Look we don't donate to anybody! I'm tryin' like hell to get the funds for the golf outing and you're lookin' for a handout! I don't give a damn about your kids—I'm just tryin' to get my company in the black. Maybe next year." The owner looked down at his desktop and waved the man away.

The man leaned over toward the owner and spoke slowly,

sternly and clearly, "You walked around last month, shaking your employees down, one by one, for donations for some greasy-palmed, on-the-take, corrupt congressman. The time before that, the shake-down was for your wife and her sleazy, grease ball cousin who heads up a front called 'Save the neighborhood or I'll kick your ass' and this is your response to a legitimate cause?"

The owner gripped his pen like a knife and made stabbing motions at his desk as he said, "Out of my office NOW!" He stopped suddenly and gritted his teeth. "Oh, let me give you some advice. GROW SOME HAIR!!! FRICKIN' SANTA NEEDS HAIR!"

As he is turning to go, the man smirks as he spots an electric shaver on the top shelf of the owner's bookcase. He grabs it. In a second, he jumps around the back of the owner as he shuffles some papers, grabs him in a headlock, and turns on the shaver.

"Here, you self-serving slob; join the Marines!"

As the priest begins to step back, the figure hears creaking footsteps and turns around.

"I shaved him."

"Excuse me?"

"Never mind." He shakes his head. "I guess I've developed an attitude."

"I'm not sure I understand . . . I noticed the light on. I didn't mean to disturb you." The priest smiles apologetically as he begins his exit.

"No, Father, wait. I've been thinking." His voice begins to amplify, "I have developed an attitude."

He turned to look at the priest and the glow of the candle suggested a small ivory halo around his bald head.

That glow became the brightest on the island, while impossible as it seemed, the night grew even darker. The lighthouse did not light, and the light switch for the cell house hallways could not be found. The only lights came from the bay. The prisoners, who struggle for that glimmer of hope, only look toward the water, where the lights shine brightly. It only makes them lonelier.

Most prisoners have trouble sleeping their first night here. Someone even trains himself to sleep with his eyes open.

The man with the golden tooth wakes up in a cold sweat after dreaming he is the Birdman of Alcatraz, standing naked atop a rocky ledge with birds pecking at him. Feeling like pins are stuck in his body, he panics. He rolls out from his bed, blankets wrapping his body, and stumbles out of the room. The hallway is pitch black, and he careens off of the walls like a pinball. He finally bolts through the outside door, and stops a few feet beyond the prison entrance. Bending down, he holds his knees and tries to catch his breath. Once his breathing slows, he gradually feels the blood flowing back into his body. His eyes are now focused straight ahead, gazing across the darkened waters but seeing nothing, except the reflections from the lights that are pointing out on the water.

He begins to question—why did he hang onto the boat? What must he do now? What must he do here? Who are these prisoners? He recalls a netflash announcing the reopening of Alcatraz, but that was months ago, he barely remembers any details. No matter what, he now knows he must assimilate with the prisoners. Another question suddenly crashes into his thoughts, just as suddenly as the waves of the water are thrust against the rocks. Which life is worse, that of a fugitive or prisoner?

No matter, he is here now and he will survive.

Along with his self-assurance, the cool, soothing ocean breeze calms him and he thinks to himself that one would not be able to tell the difference between this view and one from a beautiful condo in the Hawaiian Islands. But there is a difference. This island is a prison, the amenities are nonexistent, and the length of his stay is unknown.

Rude Awakening

It took an eternity for the second day to arrive.

The sun finally makes its way through the bars on the building's perimeter, and splashes across the condo units. Most islanders are awakened by a sudden outburst. "Ahhhhh hhhhhhhhhhhhhhhhhhhhhhhh!!!!!!"

The screams are coming from inside separate condos. They share the same frequency range, but are at different pitches. They are emanating from the mouths of those taking a shower for the first time, as the hot and cold-water taps are reversed. A few people strolling down the hall hear the painful yells, and as the original screams taper down, new shrieks emanate from the hallway. These secondary cries permeate the walls of the cell house and enter the recreation yard, where a few islanders are wandering. They join in, and the new screams now reach the perimeter of the island. These disturbing sounds will become a daily routine, not for reasons of reversed faucets but rather for therapeutic reasons.

Overlooking a cliff where the waves are violently crashing against a wall of rock, the man with the golden tooth has just heard a faint scream. He looks behind him, but sees nothing. He now turns his attention toward the bay, and the city of San Francisco, which appears so distant. His face shows tremendous anxiety, as he breathes a heavy sigh. An echo from another scream enters his consciousness, and in response, the man with the golden tooth now echoes the scream toward the city, his body shaking.

The same morning an elderly woman, also badly shaking, staggers into her bathroom. She exercises her bowels, and turns around to look into the toilet bowl. "200 grams of Columbia's finest," she says to herself as a smile appears on her face. She grabs a dustpan and scoops out ten cylindrical-shaped objects. She then carefully places them in the sink, and turns on the faucet. Rinsing them one by one, she pulls up the pellet-shaped condoms with great care. She slices them open, and empties the contents into a bowl. She sticks her nose into the bowl and inhales deeply. Her body relaxes as her eyes close. Two scoops from the bowl are poured into a mug. She turns the hot water tap, but only cold water comes out. She anxiously turns on the other tap. Hot water is now added. She then stirs and takes her first sip. Cappuccino delight.

Others are not so ingenious. In the hallways, other caffeine-addicted prisoners groan like zombies in a horror film. Caffeine, a drug, was made illegal a few years ago on all government-owned property. Some islanders shake, some stagger, and some just become more belligerent.

Later that morning the sound of a helicopter awakens many, as it descends toward the island. One of the islanders runs outside, down the path to the parade ground, and gives the helicopter the finger, yelling, "Bring some fuckin' food! We're waiting for some food, bitch!"

The pilot asks his passenger, "Where do we make the drop?"

The passenger turns to her and calmly says, "He looks like a good target."

The helicopter suddenly makes a semicircle and drops several dozen feet. Now hovering about 50 feet above the screaming man, a large crate drops from the side of the copter. The islander is looking up, but as he sees the large object falling from the sky, he suddenly becomes pale, speechless, and motionless. The crate drops about 5 feet from him and bursts open, with a few hundred assorted cans scattering, a few hitting the islander in the shins. As the pilot and passenger are laughing, the passenger grabs a megaphone and yells, "This should hold you assholes over for a while."

Those who caught wind of the "food drop" eat their rations alone in their rooms. The dining hall is empty the second night, as no one feels comfortable gathering with "A-holes." But as a few more days go by, boredom created by the isolation from society and each other drives them to the dining hall. For the first several meals no one does much talking, with the exception of the bayou chef.

Suddenly through a door to the dining hall, a large figure bursts forth with two platters of sandwiches in his hands. "Eee-ahh. We ain't got da ingredient fo Jambalaya sandwich, so we's just got generic America." He laughs as he grabs some more from the adjacent kitchen.

The crowd gets in line for this buffet of baloney and peanut butter sandwiches, and one of the islanders attempts to cut in front of another in line. The one that was cut off is furious, and opens a peanut butter and jelly sandwich and spreads it on the one who cut in front of him. A scuffle ensues for only a minute.

"Hey, if you're gonna fight, leave the line!"

"You're not leavin' till you're !@$!! heavin'!" the Voice of Discontent booms.

Another islander takes a few sandwiches, and puts a few more baloney sandwiches in his pockets. When someone in line spots this, another struggle ensues. The baloney sandwiches flop on the floor.

"Ya take any mo sandwicheez and I's wax ya ass!"

But the man counters with a belch in the other's face, and both are on the ground wrestling.

A woman behind them in line repeatedly kicks both so she can make her way through to the buffet. An elderly man in his eighties cuts in front of them all.

Conversation has not found its way into the dining hall — just cold stares. The few who are gathered in the dining hall are spread out, one on each side of every folding table.

As he is taking a bite into his baloney sandwich, a man looks across his table and yells, "What the hell are you staring at?"

But the man across the table continues staring.

"How would you like me to spread this baloney on your pasty ass?"

The man across the table just flashes a sarcastic smile.

"You son-of-a-bitch!"

Mocking him, the man across the table repeatedly thrusts his tongue in and out of his mouth. The response is a baloney sandwich hurled in his direction, with only a slice of bread hitting the target—the man's nose.

The sandwich is added to an already sticky mess that has amassed on the floor the last few days. No islander has volunteered for janitorial work. As they are leaving the dining hall, the Voice of Discontent yells, "We're gonna get !#$!! rats!"

"We need to get a dog on this island to eat up all the scraps on the floor," adds another.

"Did ya see the women—there are plenty of dogs on this island."

The bayou chef bursts through the double doors and looks around. "Whood voluntare fa washin'?"

But everyone ignores him as he quietly resigns himself to the fact that it will be him.

Most islanders are finishing up their meal. One islander, however, has amassed a cheek full of destruction, ready to explode. It comes without warning, and leaves others wondering "why." Watermelon seeds are downloaded from the islander's cheek to the barrel of his curled-up tongue, shot out in rapid-fire as his head moves from left to right. One woman is hit in the forehead and looks up in shock, a man is hit across the shoulder and in the eye, cupping his hands around his eye and screaming. Another woman has been hit several times in her hair. As the man runs out of ammunition in his left cheek, he reloads from his right cheek. During the pause one islander yells, "Hit the deck!" as he rolls on the floor. A few islanders try fleeing, but are hit in the back with the seeds.

Finally, the Cajun chef emerges from the kitchen, which is facing the watermelon man's back. The chef sneaks up behind the man, and clubs him over the head with a two-day-old loaf of Vienna bread, which is as hard as an Alcatraz rock. Seeds pour from the man's mouth as he rubs his head and staggers from the scene. The rest of his dinner companions pick themselves off the floor and brush themselves off.

"No more watermelon!" a few of the islanders chant.

As more days go by, most of the islanders are now eating in the dining hall.

"Hey, this food better not have MSG in it," a man yells at the chef.

"Das da best part!" the chef replies.

Harold is sitting alone at the end of a table when a well-dressed man with circular-shaped glasses sits next to him.

"Hi, how you doing?"

Harold just looks up and says nothing.

"Don't be down. This idea of sticking all A-holes here is ludicrous based on the statistics of the bell curve. The so-called 'normal' people would comprise the middle of the curve, about 70%, and what I term 'pain-in-the-butt' people would be bunched at one end, about 10%, of the population. At the extreme end, the real A-holes make up 2% of the population. I should know, I'm a statistician. So considering the population of San Francisco, that's still in the magnitude of several thousand. You're probably saying to yourself, 'then why are there only 200 people here? Are we the extreme cases?' I think not!"

Harold just glances at him and says nothing.

The actuary adds, "I'll tell you why. We were just the first ones caught."

After a long silence, he continues "There are thus fewer A-holes, thousands fewer here, than in the rest of America. Fine, I'd rather be here. Have you noticed the ethnic and racial make-up of the people here as opposed to America in general? Percentage-wise, there's a lot less . . ."

Harold then yells, "Shut up, motor mouth!" He then leaves the dining hall.

The actuary mutters to himself "What an A-hole."

A few tables down an unshaven man with crumpled clothes belches out loud. No one is sitting next to him. A woman a few feet away from him at the next table says sarcastically to another woman, "Boy, I wonder why he's here. I was behind him going into the dining hall. He didn't hold the door open for me—he let it slam in my face."

The other woman adds, "I know. At first I was sitting right next to him at the table. Then I noticed a bad smell. I wasn't sure if that big boy let out gas or it was just his body odor. I had to leave the table."

The first woman responds, "It probably was a combination of both. Couldn't that 'Big Boy' eat without making such loud noises?"

The other woman belts out to the islander next to her, "Speaking of pigs, which ones built these units? There's a cemented booger on my shower wall. Disgusting!"

Another jumps in "Yeah, they even forgot to put a handle on my toilet. I had to rig my hair brush as a handle."

"What about the walls? I have to stare at gray walls because they didn't paint over the drywall."

"We should file a petition with the mayor!"

"Uhh, numbnuts, he's the one that put us on the Rock."

At another table, one man whispers to another, "They confiscated my beer maker. All they let me bring here is this yeast and beer mix." The man then pulls two packets out of his pocket.

The other man whispers back, "You don't need that mixture. I can make you some beer." He puts his cup on the ground, stands up facing the corner of the room, and unzips his pants. The first man looks horrified as he hears splashing. The second man lifts the cup from the ground and offers it as he laughs, "Here's some homemade scotch ale, with a head on it." The first man immediately leaves the dining hall in disgust.

At another table a man is overheard saying, "In my opinion, Republicans should be here exclusively. They're the biggest A-holes."

The man sitting next to him laughs, "How about small-breasted women?"

A man many seats down joins in, "How about small-breasted Republicans?"

A woman sitting at the end of the table says to them, "Only guys should be on here. They're all A-holes!"

All the men start laughing, except one, a grimacing, red-haired young man. One of the men elbows him and says, "What's eatin' you? The food?"

He pounds the glass on the table, jumps out of his chair, and slams the chair into the table. One person at the table moves back and says, "Howdy Doody's late for the big show."

At another table a man points out, "Hey, my neighbor, he's

the biggest A-hole. I think they took sympathy on him because he's in a wheelchair. But then I get in trouble for making his wheelchair pop wheelies."

Another responds, "Well, there's no wheelchair access on the island. They made other exceptions. You'll notice there's also no single moms here."

"Yeah, they didn't want to foot the bill for day care. Who's gonna take care of snot-nosed Timmy when his mom's suckin' gravel in the prison yard?"

During the discussion someone asks, "Hey, did my sandwich move or what? Are these tables crooked?"

The perfect time. Almost everyone's in the dining hall. She searches in a sly, slow, casual manner. As a stranger's door is softly opening in cell block "B", a head curiously peeps in. Eyes are darting back and forth into the room. On one wall the visitor sees a Chicago Cubs pennant with the year "1945" blazed across it. On the same wall is an old photo of a Cubs player, uniform number 35, swinging a bat. The visitor cautiously steps further into the room, and is disappointed with how barren it looks. The only thing of note is a collection of the latest fad in sports collectibles, the "bubblehead" collection. This intrigues the visitor, who slowly approaches the collection. She notices the tiny heads on big plastic bodies on all the figures. One has boxing gloves with "Tyson" scrolled on a plaque below. Another holds a bat with the word "Bonds" below it, while yet another is posed holding a football with "Owens" engraved on it. On a shelf below are small glass slides, each mounted on a polished walnut base. Curious, she gently picks up one of these transparent slides, on which the name "Popeye Zimmer" is engraved. She is baffled, and picks up another slide, on which the name "Fergie Jenkins" is engraved. She carefully turns it over to see the underside of the base, on which "Official DNA licensed by Major League Baseball" appears. She is still puzzled, and her insatiable curiosity drives her to pick up Fergie and put him in her pocket. Finished with her search, she decides to try another unit.

This unit is kitty-corner to the previous one, and the visitor again cautiously opens the door. As she tiptoes through the entrance, she notices a large picture hanging on the opposite wall, tilting to one side. As she approaches the picture, she sidesteps over a pair of boxer shorts. The picture is that of a little league team huddled together. The coach is smiling, standing in the center of the children. Hmm . . . The coach's face looks familiar. As she moves closer toward the picture, a cheer jumps out.

"Go, mighty Athletics!
We never give up, we put up a fight!
Go, mighty Athletics!"

"What the?" She quickly steps back, and as she does so the motion-activated cheering stops. Underneath her feet she feels the crackling of glass. Looking toward the adjacent wall, she sees another picture. Cautious not to get to close, Tricia squints at the portrait. The glass on the picture is cracked down the middle and the corner of the frame is chipped, but she can discern a couple with their arms around their child.

It's a typical family pose, with all smiles beaming, yet broken through the glass.

She now turns to the left and sees an assortment of clothing items scattered throughout the room. There's an orange sweatshirt draped over the bedpost, blue sweatpants over the chair by the desk, and a grey blazer balled up in the corner. She gently strides toward the desk, and notices a few objects. Her eyes first catch a wooden car model, and a tiny trophy next to it inscribed with the words "1st place–Pinewood Derby." Closer to the bed is a Bible, with a rosary draped around it.

She turns toward the bed and sees a small tube lying on top of the ruffled sheets. Her pace quickens to match her curiosity, and she springs onto the bed, grabbing the tube. "BENGAY"? She tosses the tube back onto the bed, and wipes her hands on the orange sweatshirt nearby. As she steps from the bed, her eyes see a pair of prizes. Two pieces of luggage. She swiftly opens up one piece, but it has already been emptied. She attempts to open the second piece, but it is shut tight. She shakes it back and forth, and bounces it on the ground. No luck. She bangs it against the bedpost, and moves it back and forth toward her. Finally it springs open, and a jock strap from the luggage jumps on her lap.

"Ahhh!" She falls backward and shakes her head in disgust as the yellowish supporter falls to the ground. This completes her tour, and as she is leaving, she suddenly stumbles across the room. She looks back to see what caused the loud clanking noise. A toolbox is lying to the right of the entrance, along with various pieces of large pipe. Fear has now taken over, as she thinks someone may have heard her stumble. She scurries out of the room, running back into her own unit.

Once in her unit, she positions a chair under her doorknob and ties a string from the doorknob to her bedpost. She pulls out a pocket drill from her purse, and bores a hole at eye level in the door. A bottle of glue is retrieved from her purse, and she spreads it around the inner circle of the hole. Again, she pulls out an object from her purse, and sticks it into the hole. The eyepiece for the peephole fits perfectly.

Her breathing slows as she says to herself, "Keep your eyes on the prize."

Jobs

As spring progresses, the necessary supplies are dwindling. Some islanders run out of their rolls of toilet paper. At the dining hall one morning, more than a few islanders are grumbling at breakfast time.

As one of the islanders scoops a pork sausage in his mouth, the Voice of Discontent stands up and yells, "I got no !@#!! toilet paper to wipe my ass." As he looks down at his plate, he yells, "What am I supposed to use, these !!$#! crepes?"

The old woman next to him scornfully says, "I already used them."

The Voice of Discontent then flips the crepe over with his fork to examine it.

The actuary stands up and says, "I think we better go easy on the water. After observing the drinking habits of the inhabitants, I did some calculations."

"Easy on the water? How 'bout easy on the ?#@$!!! hot sauce!" adds the Voice of Discontent.

The actuary continues, "I divided the total water supply by the total number of islanders, multiplied by their average water consumption per day to derive the number of days we can go with water."

"What are you rambling about?" another voice yells.

He raises his voice as he continues, "We're going through water twice as fast. We'll be out of water by July 12th, midnight."

"Get the hot sauce out of that chef's hands!!!"

As the Cajun chef overhears the conversation, he quickly descends to the supply room in the basement, arms loaded with bottles labeled *Smokin' Hell.*

"Somebody better order more water—now!" the Voice of Discontent yells.

The man sitting next to him says, "Who's in charge of supplies?"

No one answers.

"Listen, I'm gonna get the list."

As he rips it from the door, he yells out, "Supplies . . . Captain Zero?" He shakes his head from left to right. "Which one of you idiots is Captain Zero?"

"Everyone here's a zero, can you be more specific?"

He looks up and asks, "Who wants to order supplies?"

Another voice adds sarcastically, "I'll order the cheese balls, you order those small hotdogs."

An elderly voice asks, "Can you order me a cappuccino maker?"

Tricia then stands up and says, "I'll do it. I can handle this and the mail—no problem."

"Good, this works out perfect. When we run out of items, we'll leave a list by our door that you can pick up while you're delivering the mail each day."

The actuary adds, "While we're at it, let's write down who we have doing some of the other work. Let's just go down the list."

As they review the list, a number of ridiculous names correspond to a number of very necessary tasks. Realizing now that most of the jobs could no longer be postponed, Tricia, the actuary, and the few remaining islanders (there were a number that decided to leave at the word "work") hash out a list.

LAUNDRY .... ~~Al Capone~~
Goldie

BARBER .... ~~Bozo~~
Anonymous woman

MAIL DELIVERY .... ~~FBI~~
Tricia

RECREATION .... ~~Leo Durocher~~
Cubs fan

CHURCH SERVICES ... ~~Reverend Moon~~
Father James

THERAPY .... ~~Dr. No~~
Dr. Rench

MAINTENANCE .... ~~Machine Gun Kelly~~
Harold

LAUNDRY . . . ~~Al Capone~~ Goldie

As the three "laundry volunteers" look on the map, one of them points and says, "Here's where we're goin'."

A burly woman responds, "You idiot, 'tide gauge' doesn't measure laundry detergent." As she scans the map and slams her stubby finger in the upper-right corner of the map, she comments sarcastically, "Don't you brilliant fellas think this building marked 'Laundry' would be a good place to start?" As the words leave her lips, the cud from her chewing tobacco leaves her mouth as it lands on the shoe of the man with the golden tooth.

She booms in a baritone, "There's a spit shine for ya, Goldie."

The other man sarcastically flexes his neck and arm muscles like a body builder in competition as he looks her in the face and yells, "I'm a woman trapped in a man's body." As he wiggles his pectoral muscles, she says, "Oh yeah, then why don't ya take the next ferry out!"

Goldie just shakes his head.

They walk through the recreation yard and finally enter the laundry building.

Once there, they see brand new washers and dryers, shining when the light is turned on. The woman's eyes light up as she says, "Not bad boys, not bad at all." Ten beautiful machines, chrome plated. The other man hurls a bag of clothes in, and some of the garments fall to the ground.

The litter includes black lace lingerie from Frederick's of Hollywood, camouflage panties, underwear with a Chicago Cubs logo that has turned from blue to brown, a tee-shirt the size of a tent, a pair of long johns with a rear flap, and a pair of well-worn athletic shoes.

"Is that a pair of panties or a panzer tank?"

"Don't you dare touch those!" the woman barks as she picks up the panties.

Goldie quickly responds, "Sorry, but I'm not picking up the rest."

The other man looks around and notices a pole leaning against the wall. He grabs it and fishes the garments up one by one, with one hand on the pole and the other pinching his nose.

"There's a skid mark the size of the Sears Tower," he exclaims as he pitches the Cubs underwear in the machine. As the pole latches onto the long johns, he turns toward the woman and says in a sexy voice, "Is this your lingerie, maybe a wee-bit small?"

The woman responds with a wad of tobacco in his direction.

She barks, "Let's move it. Where's the detergent?"

While he's looking, she presses the knob in.

"Hey, it's not workin'." She starts pressing again and again, but is now punching it.

"C'mon you piece of . . ."

Goldie interrupts her and in a calmer tone of voice says, "Hold on, let me take a look at this. Relax."

"Oh, Einstein here wants to look at it."

"Uh, oh. I don't believe this!" Goldie throws his hands up and shakes his head.

"What? What? Can you make this tin can spin or not, lover boy?"

"I don't believe it. They gave us a coin-operated laundromat."

The woman starts kicking all of the machines, leaving behind a trail of dents. After being kicked, one of them starts running.

BARBER . . . ~~Bozo~~
Anonymous Woman

In the entrance to an alcove near the condos is a sign reading, "Hair Stylist In." Unbeknownst to the hair stylist, this is the same location as the barbershop that cut convicts' hair in the previous century. A spiral staircase winds down to the center of the alcove. There are a couple of wooden chairs, which face large pictures hanging on the wall.

One day as Tricia studies the sign, a young man walks out of the alcove. His hair is in a zigzag pattern. A woman in the corner then beckons, "Please come in."

Tricia answers, "Was that man's hair cut on purpose or accident?"

The woman laughs, "It's the crazy new style, you know."

As Tricia steps in, she notices the details of the makeshift barber shop. On the last few winding steps of the staircase are various utensils and sprays. There is only one source of light in this alcove, a small, bare bulb dangling from a cord high above.

"Is there enough light in here?" Tricia inquires.

"Definitely. Please sit down," the woman says.

As Tricia hesitatingly sits down, she explains, "A woman in the mess hall said you styled her hair unbelievably. We're lucky we have a real stylist on the island. What would we do here if we were stuck a year without one?"

"I'm happy to be of service. When this was one of the jobs on the list, I grabbed it immediately. Now, what do you want done today?" She stares down at Tricia's red, dye stained hands, "Looks like you could use a bleach job honey."

"Oh, no. I like the color of my hair. Just a cut today. I brought a picture of how I would like it to look."

As the stylist looks at the picture, she says, "Umm. Kind of sexy, don't you think?"

"I hope so."

Tricia's eyes are now fixed on the large photos on the wall. She then tells the stylist, "That man looks like my father. Was he a prisoner here?"

"Which one?"

"That one over there."

After a little giggle, the stylist responds, "Oh, that's Machine Gun Kelley."

"Oh, that figures," Tricia mumbles.

"That one over there is Alvin Karpis. The other is Al Capone. One guy came in here the other day and wanted his hair styled like Capone's."

"Did you do it?"

"Sure I did, honey. You have to consider the source."

After a few minutes, Tricia states, "I bet you hear some good gossip, being a hair stylist and all."

"Oh, I get my fair share. But yesterday, this guy comes in here decked out in full regalia. I mean, I'm trying to cut his hair but I got distracted by what he's wearin'. He had a 14-carat gold watch on—with diamonds loaded on it. And believe me, I know real diamonds when I see them."

Tricia's eyes grow large as she anxiously asks, "What's his name—which condo does he live in?"

"Oh, honey, I don't remember his name. But he was wearing a Loro Piana cashmere sweater—I was afraid I might get hair on it."

Tricia suddenly jerks her head as she asks, "What's he doin' dressed like that to get a haircut?"

"Oh honey, don't move like that. Please stay still; I just cut off a chunk of your hair. Anyway, I couldn't get any info out of him—he seems to keep to himself. As a matter of fact, I don't remember seeing him on the island before."

"Hmm. Was he wearing a wedding ring?"

"No. But come to think of it, he had a monogrammed handkerchief with the word 'Richie' on it."

"Richie, huh? Well, this should make for some . . ."

The woman interrupts. "Oops, honey. Please don't move. I just made a bad cut again."

At this point the woman is frustrated as Tricia's constant movements have resulted in a haircut closely resembling that of the man that just walked out of her condo.

"Well, you're all done" the woman exclaims.

"Do you have a mirror I could look into?"

"Oh, not yet."

"I know I don't have to tip for services on the island, but here."

"Oh, thank you," the woman says sarcastically as she is handed fifty cents. As Tricia leaves, the stylist switches her sign to "Hair Stylist Out."

MAIL DELIVERY . . . ~~FBI~~
Tricia

The hot water has been running for ten minutes in this lively condo. Steam is spewing from the sink, like a summer fog rolling in on Alcatraz. Tricia lifts another envelope from her mailbag, which looks like a duffel bag holding athletic gear. She looks at the addressee on the envelope, and then quickly tosses it in a pile on her table. She picks another envelope, carefully screens it, and then holds it up to the light. She squints as she shakes the envelope, but still cannot read any writing inside. She now approaches the steamy sink, and holds the letter above it. After a few moments, she returns to the table with the envelope. Her index fingernail gently slides across the glued lip of the envelope, and then abruptly halts. She retreats back to the sink, and tries a little more steam on the envelope. Again at the table, she licks her chops as her fingernail successfully makes its way through the lip. She quickly removes its contents, and reads through the enclosed letter. She shakes her head. No good gossip. She quickly licks what's left of the glue in an attempt to seal the envelope.

As Tricia reaches for another treat from her bag, the smell

of perfume arouses her curiosity. She holds the envelope close to her nose. Chanel No. 5, definitely not the cheap stuff. She repeats her procedure to steam the envelope, but it does not open, not even a bit. Another attempt, but still no luck. Frustrated, she rips the envelope open, grabbing the letter and flinging the balled-up envelope behind her. As she speed-reads the letter, her face turns red. Jackpot! With a smile on her face, she searches the floor for the envelope. But there is no sign of it anywhere. Looking at her watch, she realizes her delivery is late. She grabs an unused envelope from her desk drawer, and seals the perfumed letter in it.

Tossing all the mail from the table back into her mailbag, Tricia marches out of her room. She knows almost all the islanders by name and room now, as well as their social security numbers, the names of their pets, their places of employment, and even their blood types. She glides down each aisle, gently placing mail under each door.

On his way out for breakfast, Harold notices something stuck under his door. Suddenly his heart races, as he can barely believe it. An envelope. He races toward the door, and bends over to pick it up. No return address. Is it from his wife? Or from his son? He hurriedly picks it up, and notices a strong smell of perfume on the letter. He looks puzzled, as his wife rarely wears perfume. He rips open the envelope, and discards it on the floor. As he takes a deep breath, he begins reading.

Sweetie,
Close your eyes, and fly away from the rock.
Swoop down into my bedroom, and please help me

Unsnap my red sash, and unleash these wild beasts.
Caress lower, lower, lower,
And remove the black satin covering my chocolate cakes.
Lick my icing, and I will stroke your glowing candle.
Let me . . .

"What the hell?" Harold says to himself midway through the letter. With a look of disgust on his face, he balls up the letter, and throws it across the room. He storms toward the door and jerks it open. With his head out the door, he yells, "Who the hell has been screwing with my mail?" But the hallway is empty, and the only response is his echo.

Meanwhile, Rhonna, a young woman of unrefined beauty, has just picked up an envelope under her door. She notices that it has already been opened. With a look of concern on her face, she peers into the envelope. At first she sees nothing inside. Did someone snatch the letter? As she looks again, she sees the back of a photograph lying on the inside of the envelope. As she gently lifts the photograph, she recognizes the two people in it: her mother and herself. Her hand trembles as she breathes a heavy sigh.

In the photo she is sitting on her mother's lap, licking an ice cream cone. Her favorite was blue moon ice cream, and it colored her lips an eerie dark purple. Her mother is attempting to dip a spoon into her cone for a taste. She remembers what she said to her mom. "Mine! Mine!" as she pulled away. Her mother laughed. But the ice cream then spilled onto her dress, and also her mother's slacks, causing an end to the mother-daughter sitting pose. She would plead, "Mama, more ice cream, please."

Time has eluded both her mom and herself. She notices that her mother's hand in the photo resembles her hand now holding the photo. Her blonde hair looks remarkably like her mother's in the photo, yet growing up she never realized the vitality in her mom's hair. Her eyes, her cheekbones, her legs. For the first time, she realizes how similar she is to her mom. Yet for the first time, she also realizes there is a barrier between her mother and herself. A barrier that will last a year. A tear now falls on the photograph, and lands on the young girl's ice cream cone.

RECREATION . . . ~~Leo Durocher~~
Cubs Fan

A man with a well-worn Chicago Cubs cap and an oversized Cubs jersey is sitting on the steps of the recreation yard. He looks comfortable enough to be among the "Bleacher Bums" in the Friendly Confines of Wrigley Field. Someone is walking up the steps of the recreation yard as the fan yells toward him, "Look, it's Opening Day, let's play two!"

The man turns around as he sarcastically imitates Harry Caray: "Holy Cow! You're as senile as I am!"

As the man continues up the stairs, the fan takes out a Cubs schedule. He whispers loudly to himself, "Damn, we would've been playing the Giants today. I would've been in row 3, seat 5—my box seat!"

Goldie now struts down a few stairs and sits on the opposite end from the fan. He pulls out a pen and pad and stares straight up in the sky, in a meditative state. The fan turns toward Goldie and asks, "Do you know how the Cubs are doin'?"

Goldie then snaps out of his trance, "Uh, no. No I don't."

The fan continues, "You're probably a Giants fan."

Goldie halts his writing as he looks up. " Nah, I'm not much of a baseball fan," and continues his writing.

The fan smiles. "Well, if you were, you'd be a Cubs fan. Do you remember Banks, Beckert, Williams? Nah, you look too young. Well, let me tell you they were this close in '69." He holds his fingers close together as his squint fills the gap. Goldie nods his head apparently listening, but still writing. "Do you remember the Bartman ball in '03? Oooh, that hurt," the fan says as he moves back on the step. "The team they got this year, man, they could go all the way." He laughs as he pulls out his handkerchief and wipes away sweat. "With the pitching this year, they could finally win it all—I've been waiting over fifty years. Hey, what's your name?" he continues.

"Goldie."

"Goldie, is it hot out here? I'll tell ya, it must be the excitement. Every time I think of how close we could be to the Series, I get all worked up, ya know?" Goldie turns, smiles, and nods.

The fan stares ahead in a daydream filled with Cubs, cheers, hotdogs and home runs, "I tell ya . . . I'm dyin' to know how they're doin', he says as he crumples his handkerchief into the shape of a wrinkled white ball.

In the distance the prisoners are playing a pick-up game on the old baseball diamond. The playing field is reminiscent of the poppy fields in the movie *Wizard of Oz*. It has been growing wild and beautiful with sweet alyssum and other plants. Harold is one of the coaches. The players are approached by the new volunteer garden caretakers, who claim this is a garden and hasn't been a ball field since its old days as a Federal penitentiary. A few of the caretakers step onto the field as one says, "Look, no ball playing in our garden. This was a garden in the blueprints for the island. That's the rules."

Harold yells, "Get off the field!"

Another ballplayer yells, "Just ignore them. Keep playing."

The head garden keeper shouts, "Listen, you've already damaged some sweet alyssum. We're not leaving until you stop playing."

As a ballplayer heads toward the caretakers, another ballplayer cuts him off and says, "Ignore them. If they get hit by the ball or run over by an outfielder, it's their problem. Let 'em plant flowers with Doctor Doolittle." He continues, "Hey everybody—just ignore them."

They ignore the caretakers and continue playing baseball as one of them hits a ground ball directly to one of the caretakers. He scoops it up and says, "There, no more baseball here. You can have the ball back when you play somewhere else."

Harold, whose face has turned deep red, grabs a bat and runs toward the caretakers. The caretaker drops the ball and they all begin to run away. "He's crazy," one of them screams.

"You'll never get away with this!" another yells.

Harold yells, "We're mowing down this fag ball field!" He continues, "Let's get the mower." A few of the ballplayers head with him to the garden shed. But they notice the shed is locked, and a few try kicking the door to no avail. Harold takes his bat and smacks the lock with it, breaking it open. Harold jumps on the mower and floors it in the direction of the ball field. He has an extremely bumpy ride down the stairs from the shed to the ball field. "Damn hemorrhoids!" he screams as if riding a bucking bronco. Piloting the mower, he is zigzagging around the field in a fit of anger, cutting uneven streaks that resemble strokes from a De Kooning painting.

The 18-year old, who has been watching in amusement, laughs, "Cool, Daddio . . . except the lawnmower needs more juice!" The rest of the ballplayers join in the laughter, as the caretakers scatter. But it won't be long before they strike back.

In the middle of the night the caretakers fertilize. After playing ball the next day, several ballplayers break out in rashes.

CHURCH SERVICES . . . ~~Reverend Moon~~ Father James

Morning arrives and the church door opens once again.

"You must do two things." The priest is talking to the three new parishioners who came to Sunday Mass.

He talks in a personal way, no podium, no booming voice, and no microphone. He looks at each person individually while he speaks.

"Two things. You must give up everything you own and follow Christ, and you must have the faith of a child."

He continues, "If you give up everything you own, that is good. It is a difficult thing to let go of all of your possessions, all of those things that, in some way, mean so much. It is not easy . . ."

Silence.

". . . but give them up with faith.

If you do not have the faith of the most innocent among us—the child—then there may always be . . . somewhere in the back of your mind . . . doubt?

Yes, there may be at times. I gave up everything but I have no proof. What if . . . What if I was wrong?

Believe as a child.

Believe in God, His love, His Mother. Believe in miracles, in life, in goodness . . . in love.

You have heard the expression, 'searching for your inner child.' Go ahead, find that child and believe as he or she does.

Maybe you already do, and I can tell you this: your faith will never falter, you will not have to look back and think, 'What if.'

I know something else: each one of you here is already at least half the way there. Give up everything and have the faith of a child.

Everyone of you here has already, right here and right now, given up everything you own. It may not have been of your own free will . . . but think about it. What are you left with here on this island?"

Each person in the church looks down and around, eyes ahead but searching within.

"Almost nothing," he whispers.

The priest leans forward as he continues, "You may be more fortunate than they are." His vested arm points out toward San Francisco.

"Use this short time in your lives to reflect . . . to follow. Read about Jesus. Take His Book." He points to the five open boxes at the church exit. The sign pinned to the wall above reads, *Take two—one for a friend.*

"Read about His love. Start there and continue reading.

Read it outside, in the gentle fragrance and movement of the flowers through the grass. Read about Him in the wind through the ruins of the old buildings.

Read about Him in the cry of the gulls as they fly above the water."

The three people begin to look toward the doors and windows. They begin to look . . .

"You are found."

THERAPY ... ~~Dr. No~~
Dr. Rench

In the first of several required therapy sessions, the red-haired man spouts, "I don't belong on this island, and I certainly don't belong in these therapy sessions. My only crime has been in executing my job to perfection." He says this as he takes a drink out of his cup, gripping it tightly.

The man sitting next to him says as he laughs, "No one believes they belong here."

"No, really. Take for instance my last so-called offense. I worked for CL, you know, Certified Laboratories. I was the best stress-tester, and was hired by an acquaintance that was aware of my reputation. This one product, a new cell phone, was doing especially well with the stress test. I did all the usual — pounding the phone down repeatedly, dropping it, etc. I was frustrated at how well it was holding up. Then I pictured my old lady who used to dump on me, and before I knew it, the phone was being thrown against the wall and I was jumping up and down on it. CL had brought a school class in to show how we stress test products, and unfortunately someone reported me for screaming vulgarities and flipping off the phone. I don't remember doing any of that."

A member of the therapy session then asks, "How did the phone hold up?"

The red-haired man continues, "I later heard from my acquaintance that the company was thinking of firing me, but if they did so, they would have to pay benefits and severance. They didn't have to pay a penny by getting me on this A-hole law."

Another member asks, "What were your other offenses?"

The red-haired man squeezes tighter on his cup as he says, "All work-related. I don't want to get into it. I'll just say I had the best record for finding the breaking points of all products, from toasters to push-up bras. I think a jealous colleague did me in."

Tricia then says sarcastically, "It's always a jealous colleague, huh?" She shakes her head as she smirks at him.

The man's face color now matches his hair as he raises his voice, "I heard about you. It's because of someone just like you that I'm here." He then squeezes his cup as hard as he can and flings it against the wall as he marches out of the room.

Another picks up the cup and exclaims, "It passed the test, barring a few scratches!" Everyone laughs.

The counselor takes a deep breath as she asks, "Well, does anyone have anything they would like to add to this?" No one responds. She presses on, "Does anyone have any personal experiences they would like to share? What about you there?"

"Me?"

"Yes, you with the blonde hair. How did you come to stay here? Take us back a bit. Were you always an asshole?"

"What?"

"As a youth, did you start out small . . . you know, being a bully, starting cat fights. Did you torture small animals perhaps?"

The angry prisoner bolts out of her chair, flings her notebook across the room toward the counselor, and storms out of the session.

"Whoa! You hit a nerve with her doc. Some people can't face the past. She'll be back. But for me, for instance, from the day I got my driver's license twenty years ago, I knew I was a different breed. I remember taking up two spaces in every parking lot. No shit. I didn't even know why. It felt good! And I was always the guy puttin' the 'Kick me' sign on the backs of the nerds. Well hell, even in kindergarten I was grabbin' somebody else's nappy time blanket and blowin' my nose in it or shovin' it down my pants."

"You did that too?" another questions. "Hell, me? I was lifting up girls dresses and throwing Twinkies out the school bus window since I was this high. Man, that convertible took a beating!"

"Hey, how about this asshole move . . . when I was seven, I ran away from home for a day. I finally came back and told the police my deaf and dumb neighbor across the street kidnapped me. Hell, they're still tryin' to get him to talk!"

Chuckling, then quiet.

The counselor notices a man who seems to be in deep reflection.

"Yes?" She makes eye contact with the islander at the opposite end of the circle. All eyes are focused on him.

The man turns flush and sheepishly asks, "Me?"

"What's your name?"

"Well, they call me Goldie."

"OK, Goldie. Why are you here?"

He pauses.

"I shouldn't be here, just like the rest of you," he says as his arm sweeps the room.

A shout comes from an elderly woman in the back, "Tell us why you're here, pretty boy. Did one of your babes turn you in?"

Tricia chimes in, "Yeah, spill your guts!"

Backed into a corner, Goldie can only mutter, "What?"

The counselor shifts gears.

"Well, then, tell us what caused you to be the way you are. What was your life-changing event?"

Goldie drops his head, and wonders how much of himself he should reveal. Should he re-open his scar, or shut them off completely. Would they understand?

"Confess!" Tricia exhorts.

In an impulsive moment, Goldie clears his throat and starts to speak slowly.

"OK, OK . . . If you're asking me what changed my life, why I'm who I am, I'll tell you. She was my love, my life. We did everything together." Goldie is now clasping his hands tightly, and stares into the circle of his accidental peers. He realizes he has opened a door that he thought was locked. He hoped with all of his heart that it was locked.

"Go on, pretty boy," the elderly woman goads.

"Well, it wasn't meant to be." Goldie's voice is crackling as he continues, "I didn't see it coming. I was waiting for her . . . it was supposed to be our day."

"Go ahead," the counselor urges.

"Look, this doesn't have anything to do with me being here. Maybe we should just leave it for now."

"Give it up!" Tricia loudly demands. "C'mon, doll boy, the group is waiting."

"Yeah, I'm waitin'."

"Me too! C'mon!"

Goldie eyes the group.

"You're waiting . . . You're waiting? For what? A story? I have a story. It's not about some crazy 'I did this' or 'I hate that.' It's about a real . . . a life that could have been."

He is near tears but continues, "My heart never stopped bleeding since that day. I relive this every time I look . . ."

Goldie hears laughter and jeers from the crowd.

"Hey, maybe you didn't give her enough, you know . . ."

"Or, maybe it just wasn't, you know, up to her 'specs'."

Goldie looks at the counselor and sees her trying to hold back the laughter. He turns his head away in disbelief.

"Who are these people?" he thinks.

Harold fakes playing sad violin music with a phony, sad look on his face.

There is one person, however, that is realizing Goldie's sincerity. Rhonna is looking at him in a sad, sympathetic way. Her facial expression seems to change, looking at him, but with unfocused eyes, she is thinking and somehow appears to be looking within. Her brown eyes, flavored with a dash of turquoise and jade, slowly drop into a faraway look. All of a sudden the session is broken up with the therapist blowing a whistle. "That's it! Time! Time!" Rhonna is startled back to the present, looks up and starts blinking.

Goldie is looking at the therapist in a sideways glance of angry disbelief. They all get up and leave. Harold, with a pretend violin, keeps it up in front of his face while walking away.

The therapist, after everyone leaves the room, lights a cigar and says to herself, "What a freak show!"

Afterwards Goldie and Rhonna talk a bit.

After a moment of silence, Goldie adds, "Yeah, I got on my knees once for a woman, but I don't want to get into that now. About yourself . . . who was it?"

Rhonna responds defensively. "What!" She becomes embarrassed and guarded.

Goldie continues, "I've been with people like you, it's always something. Nobody, none of them . . . You're insecure, I know. Look at all those rings on your fingers. Look, you don't have to talk about it either. It's OK."

"You don't know me. You're not a therapist like that . . . what's her name."

"You're right. I don't know you. I'm sure I never will. I'm just saying that . . ."

"And what do rings have to do with anything? I like jewelry. It's flashy, like me!

"They are round, not broken. They stay on you; they don't fall off. You don't always notice them, but they are still there when you do. They hug your hands, they hug you."

He says in a whisper without looking at her, "They are not like glass, they can't be broken." He then looks up and says softly, "Hey, I don't mean anything by this. I'm just asking."

"If you're asking me to tell you all about me, about why I'm here talking to you . . . I don't know the answer. I'm having fun, I always liked having fun. Until this fun turned into this bullshit . . . this crime!"

"I'll tell you what's a crime. It's a crime that you're here and I'm here."

"No kidding, but people like Tricia should've been here years ago. I worked with a chick like that once. That's part of what destroyed our relationship." She stops abruptly. Goldie looks at her, realizing she stops short of revealing something about herself, something she really doesn't want to relate. He stays silent. Rhonna realizes she has been turning the rings on her fingers around, playing with them. She looks at her fingers, clutches her left hand and opens it up palm down, and looks up at Goldie as if getting back into conversation.

Rhonna continues, "What a bitch!"

Goldie motions toward the door, realizing she's thinking about something unsettling.

"Rhonna," he softly says, "when I said you were insecure, I didn't mean to offend you, but I knew it. I saw that in you, that need for attention."

Rhonna looks down in shame and embarrassment. Goldie continues, "Look . . . wait. It's something in myself, too. It's a need. But when you get the attention, you get bored. I look somewhere else too . . . for something more."

Rhonna confides, "If I was insecure, it was in the past. The distant past."

"You can always learn something from yesterday," Goldie says softly. He philosophically adds, "If there's one thing I've learned, it's never to get on your knees for anyone."

Rhonna just looks at him. While he says this, he doesn't

look at her; he just walks, and looks downward. He doesn't see her staring at him while they are walking. A few minutes pass by without an exchange of words. They set off in their own directions, off to their own rooms in the shadows of the prison.

MAINTENANCE . . . ~~Machine Gun Kelley~~ Harold

Bang! Bang! Bang!

No answer comes from inside Harold's condo.

Bang! Bang! Bang!

"What the hell do ya want?" a voice is screaming inside the room.

"The shitter's boiling over! Come quick!"

"Do you know what the hell time it is?"

"We don't care what the hell time it is. Get your ass out here!"

After a minute Harold throws open the door. Five angry faces are staring at him.

"Who the hell do you think you're t . . ."

"My shitter's boiling . . ."

Another voice interrupts, "Mine too. Do mine first."

Another yells, "No mine first."

As the pushing begins, Harold slams the door.

"Hey, open up! Open up or you won't get a damn thing to eat the rest of the year!"

Bang! Bang! Bang!

A feminine voice screams, "Open up or we'll torch the place!"

Suddenly the door swings open.

"You and you—do it yourself. You wanna play hardball, we'll play hardball. Anybody else?"

There is a long period of silence. Harold looks over at Goldie, who has been silent the whole time.

"OK, Goldie Asshole, I'll do you first," Harold yells.

Goldie's face turns an angry red, and he walks away. The door to Harold's room slams shut, and in an hour he comes out and heads toward the 18-year-old's condo.

Bang! Bang! Bang!

"Who the fuck is it?"

"Get your ass up and out. We got work to do."

After a minute there is still silence.

Bang! Bang! Bang!

"I repeat—Who the fuck is it?"

"Open the freakin' door. You signed up for maintenance too, let's go! We have an emergency."

"All right, I heard you, Cro-Magnon man."

When the 18-year-old emerges out the door, Harold pins him against it.

"Don't ever talk to me like that," he says as he releases his hold. "Let's move."

The 18-year-old reluctantly follows him to Goldie's condo.

As Harold enters Goldie's living space, he notices the condo is only half finished. There are iron bars covering half of the bathroom entrance, and he has to turn sideways to squeeze into the bathroom. As he glances back at the bars, he barks, "Hand me the hacksaw."

As the 18-year-old enters the room, he complains, "Man, it smells like crap in here."

"I'm not going to say it again. Hand me the damn saw!"

As he hands it to him, the 18-year-old adds, "Why do we have to work so hard for these A-holes? I don't see anybody else workin' so hard."

"That's the trouble with your generation."

"What?"

"Workin'. Your generation doesn't know how to get their hands dirty."

"It's not just my generation on this . . ."

"Shut the hell up and hand me the . . ."

"You know, you're an asshole, just like my dad."

"Blaming your dad? If I was your dad, I'd kick your ass."

"I should've kicked my dad's ass!"

"What did you say?"

"You heard what I said."

Harold quickly shoves the young man against the bars, and pins him up against it. His left arm holds him against the bars while his right hand instinctively grabs a wrench from his tool belt. He spins it through his fingers like an outlaw, opens it, and holds it in front of the young man's face. The teen looks into the eyes of the furious man. He stares into the anger and frustration of a man who has his life taken away from him. Suddenly, Harold forces the wrench down and around the testicles of the frightened teen. He tightens it slowly and applies more than enough pressure to make his point.

"Don't ever . . ."

A moment of silence.

Suddenly Harold loosens the wrench and pulls it out of harm's way.

" . . . talk to me like that again!"

The young man is still frozen against the bars.

"You got one second to get outta here!"

The young man leaves the bathroom and goes into the bedroom. His boots are marked with grime, and his footprints are highlighted around the rooms. He then looks around, noticing a lit candle on the end table. He approaches the table and sees papers scattered around. He picks up a few sheets and reads them, but one poem in particular grabs his attention.

I saw her there as I approached the bus stop bench.

Her brown hair tasseled, unkempt, but couldn't get a good view of her face . . . I couldn't be sure.

I was with a couple of friends today, a balmy December day. They noticed her too.

We talked and laughed as we walked over to the bank, two women, two men.

I stared, and I don't like to stare, but I tried to catch a better glimpse, to see her face.

I saw her coat, saw her stockings, her shoes, even noticed her bags.

I know she wasn't waiting, not for the bus.

I couldn't get a better look and kept walking, talking with a couple of friends.

I didn't have any business there at the bank, so I stood outside. You know, I watched her there from across the street.

From that distance, you really can't recognize a face.
But I looked. She didn't.
Her head turned to look to the left. She crossed her long
thin legs. And she sat there.
I couldn't tell, but I'm guessing she was staring, at really
nothing at all, the way you used to do.
And then she . . .
it's funny, you know,
she placed her hand on her chin, her fingers to her lips . . .
the way you used to do.

"Hey, look at this—a sensitive poem from Goldie—*she placed her hand on her chin, her fingers to her lips the way you used to do.*" But Harold does not respond.

The 18-year-old continues, "Hey, how come you're not sensitive? Maybe you could write—*he placed his hand on his pipe, his fingers to his . . .*"

As Harold finishes up the job, he yells, "I'll give you three seconds to get back in here."

The 18-year-old laughs, "Aw, you're no fun."

As the 18-year-old walks into the bathroom, Harold says, "There, all you have to do is tighten the washer and nut—do you think you can handle that much?"

The 18-year-old says sarcastically, "Yes, Commandant!"

On their way out, Goldie is entering the condo. They pass, but do not exchange words. Goldie walks into his bedroom and notices he left his poems out. To his dismay, he notices a dirty fingerprint on one of the pages.

Later that evening, the 18-year-old strikes up a conversation in the dining hall.

"Hey, do you know where I can get an X7 engine?"

A few islanders shake their head.

"Looked around the shed, but just see an old Honda engine. Need somethin' with a lot more juice than that to supercharge the mower."

More silence.

"OK, I'll just use what we have. By the way, for you 'sensitive' guys at this table, here's something from Goldie's room."

A few are snickering, and the Voice of Discontent says, "Oh, you and Goldie are an item?"

"Shut up, I was fixin' his pipe."

The Voice of Discontent jabs "Oh, I'll bet," as the others are laughing.

The 18-year-old pulls a piece of paper from his pocket and begins to unfold it, while others at the table are trying to grab it from him.

Goldie is at the next table with Rhonna, when all of a sudden the 18-year-old stands up and clears his throat as he looks over at Goldie:

"Fuckin' dynamite,
Fuckin' dynamite,
My love is like a fuckin' stick of dynamite.
When she blows, she blows real good!"

All the men at the table are howling and pounding their fists, while the Voice throws his plate of food up as he yells, "KABOOM!" By this time Goldie's face is an embarrassing purple tone, and he marches out of the dining hall.

Rhonna stares an angry hole through the men and screams, "You assholes!"

One of the men yells out in a British accent, "Me? An arshole? You've got to be kidding!" Everyone in the dining hall is laughing.

Rhonna is trying to catch up to Goldie, who strides toward the recreation yard.

"Wait! Goldie, wait!"

But Goldie picks up his pace.

"Goldie, please!" She catches up to him and tugs at his sweater. "Goldie, don't let them get to you."

As she looks in his eyes, she notices a glaze, just a moment before a tear and whispers, "Let's go for a walk." But Goldie shakes his head, and looks toward the bay as if he has some unfinished business. Rhonna tugs on Goldie's hand as she begins to sit down on the top step of the recreation yard entrance. Now both are sitting, and there is an awkward moment of silence.

"Rhonna, you didn't have to . . ."

"I wanted to let them know exactly what they are . . . sometimes there is truth in justice."

After a few minutes pass, Goldie turns toward Rhonna and says, "They must have found out I write poetry. It's an easy target for these guys."

"They're just jealous. I'd love to read some of your poetry."

"Do you read poetry?"

"Well, not really. But I'm willing to learn."

After an awkward silence, Rhonna points to the sky and says, "Look at the sun setting over the ocean. There's got to be poetry in that."

Goldie just smiles.

Rhonna continues, "Let's go by the shore and look at the skyline of San Francisco under the setting sun."

After both get up, Rhonna leads the way. As they exit the recreation yard and wind down the path, Goldie inquires, "Want to head toward the beach or farther down the trail?"

"Let's head toward the trail."

As they quietly walk down the trail to the rocky shore, Rhonna looks toward San Francisco.

"What would an artist see from here?"

"Each artist would see something different. That, by definition, is an artist."

"What do you see?"

"I see something different every day. I don't see the buildings, the skyline, the bridges. I see through them, beyond them." Goldie points toward the city as he continues. "I see things at street level; the lovers joined together on the park benches, the lonely old man in the alley, and the college kids hopping bar to bar. It's the collage of the city at any point in time. It breathes a mixture of air, both pure and impure."

Rhonna looks at him in both puzzlement and astonishment. "Tell me about the lovers on the park bench," she grins. She senses his past, and slips her hand in his, with a comforting touch. He then turns toward her as his hand caresses hers.

Goldie looks downward, as uneasiness has spread across his face. "Their love is their secret. Their story—their own."

Rhonna senses that he has turned inward, and awkwardly searches for some words. She points toward the city as she says matter-of-factly, "See that building over there, the tall one with the green light on top?"

"Which one?"

"The one next to the building with all the yellow lights."

"Yeah, I think I see it."

"That's where I worked about five years ago. I had a window office overlooking the bay."

"Really?"

"Really. At night, I remember how beautiful it was seeing the reflection of all the city lights on the water. I never noticed Alcatraz, though it was right in view." Quietly, she says, "Now the tables have turned, and I'm on the outside looking in."

Goldie returns silence as Rhonna continues, "Do you suppose anyone in those buildings ever looks here, ever thinks about us?"

Goldie shrugs his shoulders as they both head back up the trail.

Meeting at High Noon

In a crowded elevator a stern voice requests, "Fourth floor." A suited man rifles through his briefcase and pulls out a manila file folder. As the doors open, he holds it firmly in his right hand and, in a brisk pace, enters the meeting room, with his comrades in single file behind him. He opens up the door and turns on the lights.

"Mayor."

A figure, slouched on a chair with head facing the ceiling and mouth wide open, is whiplashed forward. Stopping in the middle of a snore, the figure's glazed eyes open and stare straight at his suited advisor. A few seconds later, his head falls backward to its original position. He continues snoring. One of his aides bends over to whisper in his ear, "Mayor, wake up. Wake up."

Unexpectedly, the mayor lets out a primal scream, which deafens the aide who is a foot away from him. He then grabs him by the collar and whispers, "If you ever barge in here again I'll tear your heart out." The aide cowers at the end of the meeting table, where the rest of the aides take their seats.

"Would one of you kiss-ups like to get me a cup of coffee?" the mayor barks. Three of them rush toward the open door.

"Wall safe, third shelf," the mayor yells to them.

"Mayor." The advisor opens the manila folder and places it in front of him, noticing he is wearing no pants.

The mayor yawns. "Look, I don't want to read this crap. What's the punch line?"

As they all take a seat, the advisor says, "There's been a mistake."

"Mistake? What kind of mistake?"

"There's somebody on Alcatraz that shouldn't be."

"What?"

"The Strikers took the wrong person."

"How could that happen?"

"It was crowded. They took the guy that *looked* like an asshole."

"So what's the problem?"

"Mayor, he's not an asshole."

"Is that what he said?"

"Yes. But all of them say that when the Strikers get 'em. In this case, he was right."

The mayor now rubs his eyes and stares back at the advisor.

"Why are you telling me this now? It's been three months." Silence ensues, but the mayor continues to press his point. "Well, brownies, why now?"

"Sir, you've been away on vacation the past three months. We contacted your wife, but she said she didn't know your whereabouts."

The mayor's one eye is now twitching, in a struggle between the world of consciousness and sleep. His eyebrows now rise, pulling his eyes open wider.

"Where's Jethro with the java?" the mayor yells.

"Sir, regarding the situation," the advisor softly says, "All his stats are in the folder."

A longhaired aide pipes in, "You want a quick run down? Indian Guides tribe leader. Pee-wee tee-ball coach. Knights of Columbus member. Is a volunteer for the Red Cross. Sierra Club member. He drives a minivan for God's sake! Do I need to continue?"

But the mayor's eyes are again starting to close, as he is not fazed by these revelations.

The longhaired aide adds, "Does that sound like an asshole, Mayor?"

The mayor now inhales deeply. He pans the room as he firmly states, "You're telling me that this guy was never an asshole? I don't believe it. I don't care how many damn organizations this guy's in. I've butted heads with assholes in those kinds of organizations before."

"Mayor, at least look at the spec sheets."

As he turns to the first sheet in the manila folder, he sees a family portrait. A couple, along with their two kids, is nestled together with beaming smiles. Below the portrait is information about the family.

The longhaired aide pleads, "He's been married 24 years. Two months from now is his 25th wedding anniversary."

Dispassionately, the mayor states "His wife looks like this Jew who used to live down the block from us when I was a kid. I remember . . ."

"Mayor!" the longhaired aide interrupts.

The mayor now turns to the next page, which shows a bare buttocks with a red "A" inside a black circle emblazoned on it. The mayor's expression resembles that of a punch-drunk boxer just receiving smelling salts. He quickly pushes aside the papers along with the manila folder.

"What if we leave him on?"

"You can't leave him on. You'll ruin him," the longhaired aide says.

The mayor ignores this comment as he looks toward the other end of the table. "What else? Can he or his family sue us?"

The advisor at the end of the table stands up. "We added a clause specific to this law stipulating no litigation could be pursued. It was at your request, remember, Mayor?"

The mayor nods his head.

The longhaired aide stands up straight and says, "We have to pull him off the island. Morally, it's the right thing to do. I'm sure his stay has caused some psychological trauma, but it is not irreversible yet. He still should be able to assimilate into his previous social life."

"Morally, it's the right thing to do," the mayor repeats in a slow, mocking manner.

An aide wearing thin, rectangular glasses clears his throat and says softly, "I'm not so sure. The last three months, this guy's been in the A-hole culture. If he wasn't an A-hole when he went on the island, he's one now."

"What? Wait a minute. Let me say something here." The longhaired man points his finger at the bespectacled aide and swings it across until its aim hits the mayor. "Are we going to sit here and justify keeping an innocent man in prison?"

While the longhaired man is talking, the mayor stares down at his watch.

A crew-cut aide looks sternly at the longhaired man as he says, "If you feel so strongly, why don't you swim over there and search for him among the 200 A-holes. But grease up your body for the swim."

The longhaired man's face now turns a shade of red. He starts to make a point but is ignored. The crew-cut man continues, "I can't talk with this radical next to me."

"I demand to make my point," the longhaired aide shouts.

The others around the table look uncomfortable. The bespectacled aide does a "Rodney Dangerfield" with his tie. The lone woman at the table is snapping her bra strap.

Not fazed by his colleagues, the longhaired man continues on his rampage. He looks directly at the mayor and snaps, "We need to immediately develop a strategy to get him off the island."

The crew-cut man looks at everyone in the room and says, "We need to develop a strategy to get you out of this room."

"I'll second that," the mayor says as he leans back in his chair.

The longhaired man pounds his fist and sweeps his hand across the table, knocking some files and cups on the floor. "You'll have to drag me . . ."

Before the man finishes, two armed security guards burst into the room and head toward where the mayor is pointing. As they grab the longhaired man, he screams, "This is the last straw, Mayor. I quit!"

After the guards haul him out, the mayor leans forward in his chair. "Number one, quit snapping your bra strap, Vera. It's making me nervous. Number two, see that the guy doesn't talk."

The crew-cut man quickly adds, "No problem, he will have a history of mental illness."

"Number three . . ." But before the mayor can finish, his aides come back with his third demand. As the mayor sips his coffee and reaches down to scratch his crotch, he says, "Now, where were we?"

The woman pulls back her hair and says, "If you take him off the island, you'll expose this system as a flawed one. The press will jump all over it. The press will turn the tables on who the A-holes are."

After a minute, the mayor continues, "Let me get this straight. If we leave him on the island, he's the asshole. If we pull him off, I'm the asshole." The mayor now stands up, turns around, and continues, "And I think I can show you that I'm not the asshole." As he starts to pull down his boxers, a chant of "stop, Mayor" arises, along with a rapid succession of bra-snapping noises.

"Mayor, sir, I've had my fill of cellulite this morning from my wife."

"Do we have to salute this?"

"Salute Alcatraz!"

The mayor, still holding the elastic band around his underwear, makes an about-face with his buttocks now facing the window.

"Henry, get the blinds!" the mayor exhorts as his advisor rushes over to the window to follow his orders. He backs up to the window. Now inches from the window, the mayor peels down his shorts and bends over. His buttocks now bounce against the window, and in reaction he moves a few steps away from it. A spontaneous combustion of laughter arises.

The bespectacled aide snickers, "Did you feel the room shake?"

The advisor, realizing what is happening, stands up and points to a roomful of people behind the mayor. "Wrong window! That's the budget meeting!"

Spring to Summer

A figure leaves the cellblock early one morning, and heads for the isolated beach on the southern border of the island. A golf club is slung across his shoulder. As he reaches the beach, his eyes glance across the sand and focus on a large, plastic container. He smiles and his pace quickens as he approaches the bucket of balls. He pulls a tee out of his polo shirt pocket, and places a ball onto it. He slowly measures his shot, and then swings through it. It slices far to the left, and disappears into the choppy waters about 300 feet away. He attempts the same shot, but the ball slices a bit less this time. He repeats the above routine several times, as the ball lands closer to the opening in the bay, the hole in his mind's eye. With his last ball, he turns his back toward the waves and takes a swing. The small white dot sails through the air and lands between the cell house and the recreation center. "Yes," he whispers to himself and with a squint, "I think it landed a little bit closer to your suite, Mr. Mayor." On his way back to the condo, his eyes shift back and forth between the rocks and scan the island and its buildings, the way a thief sizes up his next target.

"Nice shot, sir." A figure in a grey jumpsuit startles him in deep thought. The golfer looks up and smiles.

The figure in the jumpsuit beckons, "I think you might want to see this, sir."

Puzzled, the golfer makes his way to a yellow tripod standing near the figure in the jumpsuit. Through the scope on top of the tripod, the golfer observes a stranger in the lighthouse.

"Can I zoom in a bit closer?"

"Sure, sir." The figure in the jumpsuit approaches the tripod, but the golfer waves him off.

"Never mind. I have it."

The stranger in the lighthouse is also looking through a telescope, and appears to be connected to it as one entity. She is rotating the scope toward the northern part of the island, and apparently hasn't discovered the golfer, who has seen enough.

"I didn't know there were watch guards on this island, sir."

"There aren't any." A smile covers the golfer's face.

"Mr. Harris, I know this is none of my business . . ."

"You can call me Richie."

"Yes, sir. I was wondering why your firm hired me to survey this island. Don't get me wrong, I appreciate it very much."

"This is one of my business projects."

The man looks puzzled, as Richie winks and quickly turns toward the cellhouse.

"One more thing, sir. I mean, Richie."

Richie then stops in mid-stride and turns toward the surveyor.

"I'm surprised to see you here. I was a bit apprehensive myself coming to this island, considering the prisoners and such."

"I'm just doing my homework. Don't worry, I'm well taken care of."

"Thanks for the transportation. You really do have carte blanche in this city."

Richie smiles and continues on his way toward the condos, and the surveyor quickly folds his tripod and heads toward the edge of the island.

As Richie has his ritual every summer morning, so does the stranger in the lighthouse. She has a set pattern of where to point her scope and at what times. She first shifts the scope around the perimeter of the island, from the pier, the barracks, around the Agave Trail, to the rocky beaches. Then she works her way toward the inside of the island, from the chapel, the warden's ruins, to the cell house. She repeats this process, hoping for a "catch," to see the unsuspecting prisoners in compromising situations. She does not notice the sparkling ocean waves, the blossoming trees and flowers, or the robin's-egg-colored sky. The skyline of San Francisco has eluded her, which, on different days, has taken on distinct characters, from a mysterious woman on misty days to a circus strong man on sun-soaked days. What perspective might a poet have from this perch? Or what might a different islander have perceived from this vantage point? She is one who will surely never know.

Although the golfer and all of the island's beauty eluded her on this particular day, she still finds a few catches. As she swings her telescope toward the Agave Trail, she notices a contraption emerging from the bushes. Not sure what to make of this, she adjusts the telescope for a close-up, and two large wooden wheels fill the view. The wheels support a large wooden frame, which has a lever and cloth slung seat. A catapult! But what's it doing on this island? She nervously adjusts her telescope a bit more, and notices a figure pulling the front of this contraption.

The figure is stout, with rippling back muscles and short black hair. The sweat on its back appears to be mixed with mud, and the hulking figure appears to effortlessly move this large catapult. She is puzzled, not recalling anyone on the island matching the figure.

Tricia begins to fantasize. It's been a long time since anyone held her. Those rippling muscles that could wrap around her body, she could taste the sweating flesh. Running her fingers through his hairy chest, licking his pectoral muscles. She would slowly move lower down his body, and remove those camouflage trousers. Licking lower, lower, until . . .

Tricia is jolted from her fantasy as the figure suddenly turns around for a full frontal view. She makes a sudden gasp. This figure is an ugly woman, with a few teeth missing.

Tricia feels her body cringe, and momentarily jerks the telescope away. She takes a few deep breaths to regain her composure. Shaken but not stirred, she once again pans the rest of the island. Her telescope now focuses on the cell house and the courtyard, where she sees a quick movement. She's having a hard time tracking this darting object. What could be moving so fast? The view from the lens shows a blonde figure, hair flailing in the wind, on a lawn tractor. Upon closer examination, she realizes it's a naked woman. What? Lady

Godiva on a lawn mower? As Tricia closes in on the figure, she see the woman laughing, with a devil-may-care look in her eyes. Her head is tilted back, and her wide-open mouth captures the exhilarating air of freedom. The red 'A' on her cheek is bouncing up and down in unison with her breasts. This is one figure that Tricia recognizes. So many questions are going through her mind. Where did Rhonna find this tractor? How did it get juiced up? And how did she get a body like that? Tricia knows she will need to get to the bottom of this.

As the telescope is darting in different directions to match the tractor, Tricia is taken aback. She looks again in disbelief. The tractor is now popping wheelies.

"Whoa!"

Tricia scans the island for any more possible "catches", but is quite satisfied finding a few today. Another day, another find.

But some summer days the fog takes away her advantage. This cool, damp day breaks her routine. Tricia is shaking her head in frustration, as she abandons her post.

Goldie and Rhonna's walk near the bay side will go unobserved this morning. Goldie stops suddenly, and whispers to Rhonna, "Can you hear the music?"

Rhonna looks startled, and stops next to Goldie. A soft smile emerges on her face as she looks all around. "It sounds like a flute, but what is it?" Goldie reaches out and she puts her hand on his palm. He leads her over a few stretches of rock, right near the waterfront, and he points toward the water. The music becomes very clear.

"There."

"Where?"

They move a little closer.

"Is that it? That rusty barbed-wired fence?"

"Yep, well, it's really the wind whipping that fence. I heard that one day while I was walking around. It inspired me, because I hadn't heard music since I've been on this island. Who would have guessed—beautiful sounds coming from something like this? Well, I sat down right by it and wrote a poem."

"How beautiful. I'll bet I could play . . ." She catches herself before revealing her past. She turns to him and says, "When will you write a poem for me?"

"It would be difficult." He adds in a Dylanesque voice, "You're so easy to look at, but so hard to define." He now holds both of her hands, whispering, "The mist, the fog. You look like a figure from a different time and place."

Goldie looks into her eyes and tries to see her. Rhonna looks back, remembering a different time and place . . .

There was a room, large and empty, except for one figure sitting cross-legged on the hardwood floor. The light from the windows behind transformed it into a smoky silhouette.

A guitar lay across the legs of this darkened life, as the door to the room slammed shut. Not seen . . . only heard.

There was a moment of fleeting beauty in this female form. Her arms stretched across the instrument, while her head bowed down and her hair lay across the strings. A homage?

Suddenly, as if the sound of the door replayed in her mind, her head lifted up toward the ceiling, eyes closed, tightly, as a look of solemnity withheld the pain. Her head bowed again while the long hair glanced over the strings. In a stilted motion, her hands moved toward the guitar. Her head rose ever so slowly, but her eyes never opened. The tear that fell upon one of the strings was scattered into a thousand as she began to play.

Her eyes never opened.

The silhouette reappeared to play a classical piece, an original composition that danced and played, prayed around this empty room. For an hour. For five minutes.

She looks at him a little perplexed, but with a slight smile.

He continues, "Look out there. Doesn't the ocean seem endless? You can't even see the Golden Gate Bridge. Time never passes on a day like today."

Time was lost.

"This fog . . ." As he turns his head he continues, "I can barely see our apartment."

"Apartment?"

This was a swan song. In her world, two things would never, could never, happen again.

She would never be hurt again.

She could never play again . . . a singular being, smoky and lost, was finally revealed.

Goldie notices her hands have loosened around his, and she appears distracted. He slowly releases her hands but continues to look directly into her eyes. Minutes pass in silence, until she catches up to the present.

"The fog isn't too heavy, I can still see your face" he smiles.

"My face?"

But her eyes are looking past Goldie into the distance. He now notices the silence.

"Do you wanna head back?"

She suddenly turns her attention back to Goldie.

"No, no. Let's get closer to the water."

"Watch out, we don't want to go over."

Rhonna takes a few steps forward, bends down to pick up a stone, and then flings it.

"Did you hear that?"

"No."

"Here, you try it" she says as she places a stone in his hand.

He tosses it, but just barely.

"I heard it bounce off the rocks. Did it make it into the ocean?"

"Naa."

After a few moments Goldie echoes, "Do you hear those seagulls?"

"Oh, I didn't notice them before."

"On a day like today, sounds take over."

"What day is it?"

"Not sure. Does it matter?'

"Not on a day like today."

The Princess Kept the View

Goldie and Rhonna now expand their time together to include after-breakfast and after-lunch walks. Their first, on the Agave Trail, meets with resistance.

As they approach the entrance to the trail, the homely woman, dressed in army fatigues with a dirty camouflage T-shirt, is sitting with her back leaning against a large oak. It's impossible to tell where the camouflage pattern ends and the holes begin. She is using a Bowie knife as a toothpick.

Goldie and Rhonna try not to make eye contact with the woman, and Goldie grabs Rhonna's hand to pull her behind him in an effort to step around the stranger. She spits a piece of mortar a few feet in front of them, and their pace quickens.

"Hold it! Where do you think you're goin' with that sexy little thing?" She puts her foot out to block their path.

Rhonna looks disgusted at her and says, "Who's this carnivore?"

"C'mon, let's go," Goldie answers, still avoiding eye contact.

"Can't go here, this trail ain't open until September. Can't you read the sign?" as she points to an old weathered sign that's lying on the ground, half covered with brush. Suddenly, she flicks her wrist and the silver flash of a knife blade zips past Goldie and into the piece of wood.

Goldie says in a broken voice to Rhonna, "C'mon, let's go back."

The stranger then comments, "Now you're using your head."

She bends over to extract the knife from the sign, and as she does, Rhonna yells, "Now I'm using my foot!"

She gives a swift kick to the well-fed rear of the stranger, and the stranger tumbles over the sign. Rhonna grabs Goldie's hand and says, "Let's go," as she prances onto the trail with Goldie close behind.

They are now a safe distance from the stranger and have slowed down, when all of a sudden they trip and fall to the ground, with Goldie landing on top of Rhonna. They look back and notice a steel trip wire stretched from one tree to the next. They chuckle as Rhonna says, "Ow, ow, my butt."

"Are you all right?"

"Ow . . . I don't know," she laughs as they enjoy the accidental intimacy of the moment.

"Goldie?" Her voice lowers as she pulls him closer until his body is tight against her own. She takes his hand and slowly glides it beneath her buttocks as she whispers in his ear. "Why don't you check, you know, just to make sure."

She closes her eyes as they begin to kiss feverishly.

Suddenly, an echo covers Alcatraz like a cloud, "Ah, ha, ha, ha, have a nice 'trip'! Ah, ha, ha, ha!"

The echo reaches the summit of the lighthouse, where Tricia quickly turns her head toward the sound's direction. She peers through her telescope perched on the ledge, and rotates the scope until its crosshairs zero in on the source of the commotion. Two pairs of entwined lips are at the center of the view. She zooms out a bit to capture the identity of the couple, then picks up the logbook beside her and scribbles in it.

She peers again and suddenly becomes distracted with another sound, that of a loud slam emanating from the entrance to the lighthouse. This sound, almost directly under her, prompts her to redirect the telescope downward. As she maneuvers the scope on the uppermost guardrail, in her excitement it manages to slip out of her hands and roll off the rail. The telescope bounces off the rail and heads downward. A short moment later a scream from below is heard throughout the island. She jumps backward, with palms suctioned against the glass lantern enclosure. She remains still, terrified of being discovered. Hearing a growing commotion below, she nervously ponders her next move. As the clamoring increases, Tricia begins to move across the glass in the direction of the hatch.

Meanwhile, directly below her, within the depths of the lighthouse, the shadow of a bent figure is maneuvering its hands, twisting and turning the tentacles of the tower. The shadows follow one hand rotating left, while the other moves back and forth like a piston. Out of the shadow steps Harold, wiping the grease off of his hands. He glances down into his utility belt, looking for a screwdriver. He had been trying to make this lighthouse operational the past two days, but to no avail. Harold grabs a Phillips screwdriver and moves back into the shadows.

As Tricia turns her head toward the hatch, a sudden blast of light blinds her. She lets out a shocking scream and covers her eyes. Seconds later, another scream, as the blazing light begins its next revolution and penetrates through the openings of her cupped hands. She jerks to and fro, as if the victim of shotgun blasts, while the powerful beam of light continues to circle Alcatraz.

A crouched, erratic silhouette of Tricia is seen by the crowd below. "That's the one!" a man cries as he stares upward. "It almost fuckin' killed me!"

Soon a few dozen spectators turn into a hundred. Meanwhile, responding out of fear to the screams, Harold hurries up the creaky steps.

Tricia falls to the lighthouse deck and gropes her way toward the hatch. More taunting is heard from the angry crowd. After a few unsuccessful attempts, she finally grasps the handle and opens the hatch door. Still sight-impaired, she feels her way down the first few stairs. She is startled by Harold's booming voice from below. "It works!"

She loses her footing, but momentarily regains her sight on the way down, just long enough to realize she's soaring ninety miles an hour downward into Harold's screaming face. She clumsily lands in his arms, and the staircase sways with the impact of both bodies as they try to maintain their balance. With each additional movement, the fragile staircase swings wildly. He begins to hurry up to the deck before it collapses. A moaning Tricia still in his arms, he staggers up through the hatch, carrying her toward the railing. With two silhouettes now beaming from the top of the tower, the crowd of a hundred soon turns into a raucous mob. As the sun sets, the twilight gives the scene an eerie, Frankenstein-like quality.

"It's Kong. He's got the girl!"

"Kill the monster!"

"He's insane! Get the girl—he's insane!"

Using tiki lamps as torches, more people crowd the base of the lighthouse.

"Burn the lighthouse! Burn the monster!"

Harold looks down at the crowd, as he loosely holds Tricia's body, which sways back and forth over the railing. Tricia looks down and passes out.

"Get the rope you assholes, get the rope," Harold screams.

As the teenager answers his desperate request, the noise from the crowd grows.

"It's the coach—it *is* a monster!"

"Hey, we'll only let you down if you build us a sports bar."

"I want a Jacuzzi."

Harold drops Tricia aside. The light continues to rotate as it picks up a shadow and flashes it into the now-darkened sky. Ominous and bold, it can be seen from the shores of San Francisco, where a voice in the street yells, "Look, the bat signal!" as he points toward the sky.

Back in Alcatraz, someone in the crowd points upward and yells, "Look, it's the fat signal!"

The teenager returns with the rope, and ties a noose in it. He attempts to hurl it up the tower, but it falls far short of the railing, which is 84 feet above the ground.

Harold retorts, "My fourth-grader can throw farther than

you. Ah, screw it!" Realizing it's up to him to get them down, he shields his eyes as he bounces back and forth between the railing and the lamp. Finding the hatch door, he begins to descend the shaky spiral staircase. Tricia begins to regain consciousness as the jeering mob becomes louder. She once again crawls to the open hatch. She yells, "Hey, help me," as she sees Harold struggling to keep his balance on the violently swaying staircase. Ignoring her, he continues to descend. She attempts to grab onto the railing, and finally succeeds. She struggles to keep her footing, and is like a toddler learning to walk.

A voice in the crowd yells, "Hey, where day go?" Silence befalls the crowd.

Inside, Harold is sweating profusely, as he now nears the last tier of stairs. With each step he takes, the stair gives way. He grips the railing tighter, and is now sliding down the collapsing stairs. As the railing breaks away, Harold swings downward like a screaming Tarzan, and after losing his grip, lands on his derriere. While Harold rubs his aching buttocks, he looks twenty feet above to answer a call for help. He sees Tricia on the upper part of what remains of the staircase, which is swaying like a pendulum. Her face is frozen in horror at the void where the staircase used to stand.

Harold hollers, "Jump!" as he holds out his arms, but she is still frozen on the staircase with a death grip on the railing.

"Pry your butt off the stairs and let's see that cellulite shake!" Tricia doesn't move an inch—she is in shock. "C'mon, bitch, before the whole staircase gives way!" His voice becomes louder "I'm giving your fat face ten seconds to go for it—10, 9, 8, 7, 6, 5, . . ." Becoming impatient, Harold yells in disgust,

"Screw it!" as he looks toward the exit.

Suddenly a loud crack sounds from above Tricia. Hearing the crack, she snaps out of her trance, bolts off the stairs, and sails downward. While in midair, she sees Harold hurrying toward the door, leaving her to land in a pile of rubble.

As Harold makes his way out the door and enters the crowd, an airborne telescope zooms past him and crashes against the cement lighthouse. As Tricia hears the shattering noise, she falls back and moans in defeat.

Golden

He couldn't wait to get up each day to meet with Rhonna. It didn't matter where. It could be the Agave Trail or the military morgue for that matter. Nothing like before, nothing like it used to be. In his past, everything was planned, everything had to be perfect. All of the rendezvous had to take place in some deluxe hotel suite overlooking some spectacular view, the fancier the better.

Atmosphere, for all practical purposes, meant everything as he was moving in for the kill. It was also, all but a handful of times, the only beauty that was left when he awoke the morning after.

Not any more.

Now, he was being transformed.

He could hardly believe it.

He was no longer lonely. It happened in a place where so many people must have visited the depths of solitude and loneliness. This was a prison with cells, meant for the ultimate in human isolation. Rooms of solid cement and iron, no windows, no bars, not the smallest ray of light.

Artists love irony.

Poets love irony.

Goldie grins, and then gets dressed to see Rhonna. He is decked out in black. His shirt, shoes and pants are a contribution from the clergy. His pink comb is a contribution from Rhonna. And his blue windbreaker with a large, white number 38 is a contribution from the Cubs fan. With a smile, he gazes into his cracked room mirror until a bright, gold beam flashes back to him, courtesy of his tooth. Now he is ready for his walk.

This after-breakfast walk starts out differently, as Goldie sees a man bent over near the shore, with his bare buttocks aimed at San Francisco.

Goldie inquires, "Why is he doing that?"

Rhonna whispers, "I heard his wife turned him in. Every day at sunrise he flashes her the ol' tattoo."

"What tattoo?"

Rhonna giggles. "What do you mean, 'what tattoo'?"

Goldie returns a puzzled look.

"You know, the same as everybody's here."

Goldie still looks baffled.

"Well, you had to get one. Didn't you? Oh, I get it." She stops and moves toward Goldie, placing his hands on her hips as she swivels playfully, "You're just trying to get me to show you my tattoo."

A pause. "Ohhh . . . that's the mark that all these prisoners have been talking about."

"Yeah, and I suppose you're the only one they didn't tattoo?"

"Look, I guess this is as good a time as any to tell you. I shouldn't really be here."

"Everyone says that."

Goldie insists, "No, I mean that. I never told anyone, but I might as well tell you."

A scared look transforms Rhonna's face as she asks, "What?"

Goldie continues, "Well, it's a long story."

"Please tell me. It'll be our secret."

After a long pause and a deep breath, Goldie continues, "I failed miserably trying to make a living as an artist and a poet. Our society does not value true art. Well, anyway, I needed money bad, and the opportunity came at the right time."

"What opportunity?" Her hands now take his as she squeezes tightly.

"Well, through a friend of a friend I was introduced to the Cuban cigar market."

"The Cuban cigar market? That's illegal!"

"Yep. Fifteen years in prison. If you kill someone you would get about half that time in jail. When I saw them coming after me, I swam toward the boat and hung on for dear life, not knowing that I'd end up here."

"My God! What if they find you?"

A long silence ensues, and then Rhonna buries her head in his chest and wraps her arms around him.

"I'll never sell again, I'll never . . . even if I have to go back to being a shoe salesman."

As Rhonna embraces Goldie, she assures him "You'll be OK. Everything will be OK. "

Goldie returns her embrace, and several minutes go by in silence. As Rhonna lifts her head from his chest, she interrupts the silence.

"I never told you . . ."

Goldie returns a puzzled but prompting look.

Rhonna continues, ". . . why I was sent here. It's really so silly, I'm embarrassed to tell anyone." She notices his eyes are focused sharply on her. She clears her throat and continues, "I was shopping, and it's usually very boring. So I wanted to have fun with a few of my fellow shoppers. When they weren't looking, I put Slim-Fast in a hefty lady's shopping cart, a dog bone in an ugly guy's cart, and a Chia pet in a bald guy's cart."

Goldie laughs, "That's three people. Did this count as your three offenses?"

"No. That was just one. The other two took place at the beach. My friend and I were walking by the ocean, and we saw this young, obese guy. His boobs were bigger than ours. So I whispered a plan in her ear, and she thought it was a great idea. As we approached him, I winked at him and turned on the charm. As I was untying my bikini, which had an American flag design on it, I asked him if he would like to see a surprise. My friend and I were both trying very hard not to laugh; as we saw his face turn a shade of purple and his eyes bulge out. I said in a seductive tone, 'Close your eyes and count to ten.' As he closed his eyes I took off my bikini, and with my friend holding one end and me the other end, we stretched it around his chest. I quickly tied a half-hitch knot behind his back before he could even open his eyes. My friend and I laughed as the bikini could barely hold his breasts. She saluted and shouted, 'Fly the flag, fat boy!' As he frantically tried to untie the knot, I yelled, 'Lose 100 pounds and it'll drop off!' "

Goldie laughs and interrupts, "Poor guy. But how did you get credited with two offenses?"

"One was for extreme humiliation. The other was for desecrating the American flag."

Goldie continues laughing as his head tilts backwards. Rhonna looks up and sees his golden tooth sparkling in the sun. She has noticed his tooth before, but either because of her angle or the sun's, it never has reflected like this. Is it real gold? she wonders.

She flashes back to her eighth birthday, when she opened up her last present, a present from her mom. She quickly unwrapped and opened the small rectangular box, not bothering to read the card that came with it. A gold necklace and earrings set! Her best present ever. She remembers its brilliance, and telling her mom that she'll have to get pierced ears. Her mother laughed and agreed, as long as it was only her ears she wanted pierced. She ran to her mother and hugged her as she told her she was the "bestest" mom in the whole wide world.

As Rhonna now realizes she is staring at his tooth, she quickly comments, "I never told you this before, but I think your tooth is a beautiful accent."

"Which one?" Goldie naively pretends.

"The golden one. I hope you don't mind. I assume that's why your nickname is Goldie. Are you gonna tell me your real name?"

"Yeah, that's not my real name. What do you think my real name is?"

"You don't look like a Tom. You're not a Dick. And you're sure not Harry!"

They both laugh, and Goldie says ,"You're right. My name is Alex."

"That's a nice name. Yeah . . . But Goldie sounds more precious. I hope you don't mind if I still call you Goldie."

"No, not at all. While we're on a roll, I might as well tell you how I got that tooth."

As he notices her hungry eyes, he continues, "Well, when I first started selling these Cuban cigars, I sold to the wrong crowd."

"What do you mean?"

"As I handed over the 'goods,' they handed over only half the cash. When I complained and demanded my merchandise back, all I received in return was a punch in the mouth. I was knocked out cold, with one less tooth."

"How horrible. What kind of gang would do this?"

"It was no gang. I later found out it was the police."

Roses

A decaying shell. Rotted wood, metal crossbeams, and cracked cement all joined together. The ruins of the warden's house had been a symbol to Goldie, a symbol of how his life began at Alcatraz. This summer afternoon Goldie revisits the ruins. Standing amidst the rubble, he flashes back to one night this past spring, a night like many others.

Unable to sleep and sweating profusely, he pulls off his bed sheet and stumbles to find the light switch in total darkness. After trial and error, he reaches his destination. As light enters his room, he grabs a pad and pencil from his table and heads toward his bed. Scribbling on his pad, he reflects on his first few weeks on the island.

Destruction
Decay
Desolation
A fitting place for my soul
as hard as the Rock itself.

Not held together by crossbeams
or fixed on any foundation
Its strings too delicate to hold any relationships
or weather any storm.

Love and Life
once held together by the same forces
have been razed forever.

How his life has changed. Goldie now feels a lightness of rebirth in this strange land. He carefully steps through an opening in the cement, walks through some foliage, and stops by the fireplace, which is covered in ivy. His mind is creating possibilities. Maybe one night he could gather wood and build a fire for Rhonna and himself in this empty shell. Or maybe he could read her a poem by the fireplace. To him, it was the only truly romantic spot on the island.

He walks back through the opening, and takes a few steps to the garden just outside of the warden's house. Roses are plentiful in the garden this summer, a fact that has eluded Goldie until recently. A thought suddenly crosses his mind. He bends over and pulls a few petals from a rose. As he walks a few more steps, he bends over and pulls a flower from its stem, then another. With a gentle smile on his face, he heads toward the condos, anxious to begin his "poem."

Back in his room, he feverishly scribbles down his thoughts. A first attempt to convey his emotions is not quite right. A second, not yet. Goldie once again looks to the roses and colored petals for inspiration. How can he tell her? Another attempt. He shakes his head in disgust as he feels it is just not right, another piece of paper is crumpled and tossed to the floor. What will she think? After several hours, he has a half dozen pieces of paper on his table, but several dozen on the floor.

Finally, he lifts his head momentarily, as if in prayer, as he places the last paper next to the roses.

The next day Rhonna and Goldie go for a walk, down the path to the greenhouse, as Goldie suggests. He is anxious, as he imagines Rhonna's expression when she discovers his poems along the path, with roses on some poems, and petals on others. Which will be her favorite? Will she think the roses are a romantic touch, adding depth to the poetry?

As they approach the location of his first poem, Goldie's heart speeds up. A few feet away from where his poem should be, Goldie still does not see it. He stops to look around.

"Goldie, what's wrong?"

"Oh, nothing." His eyes dart around the area without any luck.

"You look pale."

"It's just that . . . Well, you see, I wrote some poems for you."

"What?"

"Yeah, I laid one down here. And another over there, and then another."

As he points his finger, in the distance he sees an old woman with a garbage pick harpooning some papers, his poems.

"Oh my God!"

He runs to her, screaming "Wait! Hold it!" Rhonna is close behind.

But she just looks up for a second and continues her garbage collecting.

Out of breath, Goldie pleads "These are my poems—give them to me!"

Finally she looks up only to scream at Goldie, "You littered this place. And it's you who picked those flowers. You're the killer. Killer!"

Rhonna yells, "Cough up those poems."

"Killer! Killer!" the old woman continues.

Rhonna rushes toward her, ready to tackle her. But the old woman throws the pick with the poems, as if a harpoon, in the ocean.

Goldie's jaw has dropped, as he is in a state of shock.

Rhonna then pushes the old lady to the ground. She bounces back to her feet and screams, "I'm reporting you to the Traz Caretakers Association. Pushing an innocent old lady down, you ought to be ashamed." Before she leaves, she spits toward Rhonna and then toward Goldie.

Rhonna yells "Innocent old lady, huh?" Rhonna takes Goldie's hand and says "C'mon, let's go," as they head toward the condos. Goldie is still in a daze as he stares vacantly toward the water.

Seaside

Hope. It was always there, but well-hidden. But it couldn't escape the long stretch of summer days, and the golden stamp of sun-soaked mornings. More islanders are discovering the bosom of the island, out and about.

How basic—all the senses working together. Goldie picks up on little things that for years eluded him, textures and smells that are part of a world he never knew existed. He thinks that this is how life should taste and feel, with nature timing the release of its elements and wonders. Forging a path in his mind, he starts his morning walk with Rhonna.

"Let's go by the Agave Trail."

"Sure."

As they walk along the trail, a long pause of silence is interrupted.

"Rhonna, when I first came here, I had a hard time sleeping."

"Oh."

"The past was too close. But lately I've been waking up at odd times in the night, and some nights I don't sleep at all."

"What's wrong?"

"Nothing, that's just it. It's for a different reason lately."

"What do you mean?"

"Look, did you ever come to a realization that shook you, that entered your core being, and made your body scream from the inside-out?'

"When my panties were too tight," Rhonna laughs.

Goldie returns the laughter and continues, "The duality of life seems more acute to me now. And at the same time, I feel more whole than I ever have before."

Rhonna has a puzzled look on her face, and glances away, in the direction of the wharf. She catches an object in her peripheral vision, and then does a double take. She glances back, and her attention is now focused on a figure at the foot of the wharf.

Goldie continues, "Besides my real name, there were other things in the past that I was trying to hide. Maybe even from myself."

But Rhonna is now intrigued by the figure, and a devious smile crosses her face.

"Rhonna, I stood at the Altar once . . ." but before he could finish, she darts out in a beeline to the figure, and Goldie's jaw drops.

She is approaching the figure as a lion approaches a gazelle. The figure, that of Big Boy with his back facing the island, still hasn't moved. She now slows down while approaching, so as not to be noticed. Then she springs into action, with a swift kick in the rear end of Big Boy. He turns around, but it's too late. He loses his footing and falls from the pier, between the wooden posts.

"What the . . . ?" Goldie yells into the distance. A frozen statue, he now realizes what has happened. He runs toward the pier, out of breath. He sees Big Boy with arms flailing in the ocean.

"Now you're ready for a wet tee-shirt contest!" screams Rhonna.

Big Boy is bobbing up and down in the water, trying to catch a single breath.

Goldie is looking for an object to throw to him, and panic sets in as he doesn't see anything.

"Let's find something!" Goldie screams in desperation.

"He should be able to float. Fat floats." Rhonna laughs.

"This isn't funny, damn it!"

Both of their eyes are on Big Boy, as he now struggles to grab a post near the pier and hang on.

"He could have drowned, what's wrong with you?" yells Goldie. "What if he couldn't swim. Why the hell did you do this?"

Rhonna looks dejectedly downward, and returns silence.

"There's some things about you that I just don't understand," he says with a quivering voice.

"I wasn't thinking."

Now both turn to see Big Boy, as he is pulling himself up from the post and onto the pier. He is on all fours down on the pier. Goldie is angry but can't help but notice that his breasts are sagging down and the wet tee shirt is stretched taut across them. This visual makes a certain part of him laugh by reflex, although consciously he avoids this impulse.

"I'll catapult your ass off this island!" Big Boy screams between breaths.

"Let's go!" Goldie warns Rhonna, as they both quickly backtrack up the Agave Trail.

After a long, awkward silence, Rhonna passionately adds, "I won't do it again, I don't know what got into me."

Goldie shakes his head in disgust. He is arms-length away from her, which is unusual.

Rhonna tries to switch gears as she back-peddles, "Goldie, what were you saying?"

"Never mind, just something inconsequential."

"No, please tell me. Something about your past."

Goldie is struggling to bring the topic back into light.

"We can talk another time, if that's OK."

"OK. I know . . . I'm impulsive. But I need more fun on this island. I'm dying here."

"But not at someone else's expense."

Rhonna is gazing forward, and doesn't say a word.

"Look, I don't mean to preach. I'm the last person that should preach. If you want some fun, why don't we do something else?"

"Like what?"

"Well, something that people who aren't prisoners do. Something people in the city would do. I know, why don't we see a movie?"

"A movie? Are you kiddin'?"

"I was walking a few nights ago and saw a light inside the barracks. I peaked inside, and saw a handful of islanders watching a flick."

"Are you kidding?"

"No, there must have been a movie projector from back in the prison days."

"Probably. I know they wouldn't have given us something for entertainment while we were here."

"Let's see a movie this week."

"What time does it start?"

"Not sure, I think they replay the same movie over and over."

"What movie?"

"Not sure."

"I'm pretty sure it's not porn, but I'll bring my 3-D glasses anyway," she winks.

Flicks

Most islanders' facial expressions are calm as they enter the building, but some newcomers have looks of anticipation. What is she missing out on? As the weeks go by, her curiosity builds.

One night she notices Goldie and Rhonna entering the barracks, holding hands. Rhonna is whispering into Goldie's ear, and Goldie laughs. Both appear to have temporarily forgotten what island they are on. Tricia refocuses the binoculars, perspiration dripping from her forehead. She zooms in and views Goldie's mouth, which is moving back and forth, revealing his golden tooth.

Goldie attempts to open the rusty door, which only partially opens. Rhonna joins him in yanking on the handle. Both are laughing as the door finally opens. They enter darkness, noticing only a beam of light in what appears to be another doorway entrance. They cautiously enter the room housing the beacon of light, and only their footsteps can be heard.

As they enter, the Voice yells at Goldie and Rhonna, "!$@%# Shhhhhhh!" Goldie and Rhonna are now looking at the target of the light beam, but do not recognize the movie being played. They see a few dozen people seated in the front rows, and spot a few empty seats at the rear, which they quickly occupy. After several minutes, Goldie and Rhonna are holding hands, with Rhonna nestling her head on Goldie's shoulder. They are now oblivious to the movie.

The Voice shouts, "Here's where she gets on the . . ."

"Shut up!" a few people yell.

After several more minutes, the Voice continues in a louder, more obnoxious tone, "Oh, this guy's gonna' take the dive! Don't do it! You stupid #@!#$%!! Watch this . . ."

A woman near him yells, "Someone tape this guy's mouth!"

Now, knowing the ending, some look at him in disgust, and a few get up and leave.

As they are leaving, another figure enters the room carrying a few buckets of popcorn. When he finds a seat, he passes the buckets to people in opposite directions. "Thanks, Mr. Bayou," one responds. After a minute, projectiles are fired from the mouth of an elderly woman into the hair of those in front of her. In the row in front of the elderly woman, another woman's hair looks like cotton candy, as it is decorated with popcorn.

Someone in the front row stands up and screams, "Ahhhhhhhhhh! Even the mother fuckin' popcorn has Cajun spice!" He tosses the bucket of popcorn up in the air.

"Son of a beech!" A few people in the front row are cursing as they get out of their chairs to pick popcorn from their hair. In the darkness they stumble into one another, as an elbow collides with a jaw, a forearm with a shoulder, and a few legs intertwine. A few fall backward and flip over their chairs, landing into the second row. The drinks that were left on these chairs splash to the ground. The cotton candy-haired woman lands on the elderly woman's lap in the row behind her. Another man is sprawled across the laps of two women, thrashing around like a fish reeled into a boat. The women in the second row scream like a banshee. A few more people attempt to leave, but slip to the ground and land on all fours. Mayhem has broken loose, and one person gets up and yells, "Who's licking my leg?"

"Stop the movie!" another yells as he turns back toward the projectionist. But the projectionist is no longer there.

"My throat is burnin'. Where the hell is my drink?" another screams.

After much pushing and shoving, cursing and yelling, and even a few thrown chairs, everyone leaves the movie theater. That is, everyone leaves but Goldie and Rhonna, who are absorbed in each other. Goldie smiles as he picks a few popcorn kernels from her hair. Rhonna does the same to Goldie, except, in baboon style, she eats a few pieces of popcorn after picking them from his hair. They giggle, and continue their embrace.

A half-hour passes and another figure cautiously enters the room, in a crouched position. She notices the screen is white. A movie reel is spinning freely, as the film has ended. Two heads appear to be glued together. She stalks closer, but still does not recognize the figures. She is now a few feet from their chairs, but as she makes her final step she slips on a wet spot, skidding halfway down the aisle.

"Whoaaa!" Her feet suddenly lift off the ground, her arms

swing wildly, and her head jerks back. Thud! Tricia is now sprawled onto the ground, moaning. After a minute, she manages to get up, holding her leg. Limping away, she utters a few unkind words.

But Goldie and Rhonna do not hear. Their lips are locked in an embrace that could last through a double feature. In Bogart style, Goldie whispers in Rhonna's ear, "This could be the start of a beautiful friendship."

Three Deadly Sins

Curiosity

The door to the condo is not completely closed. Perhaps by accident (or faulty installation), there is a split, an opening just large enough to allow a temptation. It is there; and a figure just happens to come across it, and opens the door just a wee bit more. Perfect silence is the first impression, disbelief is the next. This room is not like the other condominium living areas—marble floor, cherry cabinetry, wet bar, and fine art on the walls. Aside from all the extras on this first floor, this room is very different—clean, white with cool-blue accents. Sterile, not quite, but clean and light.

The figure can't help but open the door just a little bit more, carefully though, so as not to make a sound. The eyes widen and wander, then suddenly stop. The sofa—he just lays there on this white sofa, this man. In perfect stillness, the light from the window proves it, his limbs never move—but still he lays there in this silence, or at least what the figure thinks is silence.

This rich man is involved, preoccupied with something else. The figure knows that not because his eyes wander. Not because he looks out the window. No, his eyes are covered. They are covered with glasses that emit a subtle bluish light. It is faint, but visible. The key to his preoccupied mind is his lips. They move, and every time they do, a tiny red dot on the side of the frames flashes.

Why are his lips moving? Who is this rich man talking to? Himself? The fact is, he is whispering. Then suddenly his voice resumes its normal tone. The figure steps back, startled, then continues to eavesdrop.

"Look, honey, I've got to go. I'll see you soon. Can I have a kiss? What? You want to dance? Now?" He chuckles. "Okay, how about if we hold off on the dance for a day?" Richie pauses, then his voice changes from playful to a more urgent tone. "All right, listen . . . I've got to go see Lemond. We'll be together tomorrow; meet me in L2485, that's right! The new Lahina! That's 2:00 PM our time!"

The figure, still a bit nervous from the shift in Richie's voice and a little curious that she might be discovered, turns to sneak away—and wonders. As the figure moves down Broadway, Richie's arms begin to move, he is no longer just a blue statue bathed in white light. His arms begin to rise, then fold. He is engaged in an embrace. His hands appear to hold onto something more than air, more than what is or could have been seen by an invited guest or . . . a figure in a doorway.

Richie abruptly sits up, pulls a small keypad from his cocktail table toward him, and keys in a few numbers. "Lemond, it's good you came by. There is something I'd like to discuss. Concerning our last meeting, you were a bit 'foggy,' pardon the expression, about the actual layout of some areas of Alcatraz. Let me assure you, 'no concern.' In fact, I'll let you take a look . . . here, make sure you are on the same numbers. OK, great . . . then follow me. As you can see, I've recorded the areas of concern and as we both walk through you'll be assured that our project will map out as beautifully as it does in the preliminary blues." At the end of their conversation, Richie pauses and the red light on his frames suddenly stops. Then in an instant, another red flash as his voice raises in a subtle, almost joking question with the undertone of concern.

"Lemond, do you think *I'm* an asshole?"

Lemond replies, "It really doesn't matter, does it." The remark is made as a statement, rather than a question. "I know you like to do your research hands on, but I'll never understand why you wanted to live there now."

Richie chuckles.

"Lemond, let's touch base this Friday morning on the dimensions of the recreation area."

"OK, we need to also discuss entry access points."

"Sounds fine, see you then." Richie sets his glasses down and heads toward his wine closet. As he comes back into the room to recline with his favorite Cabernet, the space beneath the sofa catches his eye. He reaches his hand into this space, and catches his prize. Richie once again reclines onto his sofa, but this time with a grin. He uncorks the bottle, and pops open a can of Sushi Spam. He lifts it toward himself to catch a whiff, and slowly enjoys this guilty pleasure while washing it down with Cabernet. The Spam gradually disappears from the can, as does the day into night.

Ansell Roberts

Temptation

The temptation is too great. She studied his pattern. When he normally leaves with his golf clubs, how many swings he normally takes. Early this morning, she times it perfectly. From the corner of Times Square and Broadway, she sees him close the door. As she passes him, they both exchange greetings. She is now past his door, and turns to look back. No one is there. She turns around, and approaches his door. She again looks both ways. Still no one. She quietly opens his door, and, seeing no one, quickly enters his unit.

Looking around, she feels like an archeologist about to discover many treasures. But she quickly regains her focus. She reminds herself there's only enough time for the ultimate prize. She quickly walks toward the sofa, and sees the glasses lying on the cushion. She lifts the glasses up very delicately, and carefully examines them from all angles. She notices a row of unlabeled buttons around the top of the frames. She now reclines on the sofa, and gently puts on the glasses.

Nothing. She fumbles her fingers on the frames, and presses a few buttons. Still nothing. She randomly presses every centimeter on the frame, and finally a scene emerges. Her breathing is heavier now, with her heart racing quicker in anticipation. There are a few beads of sweat forming on her forehead.

She is in a hallway similar to one in the cellhouse. As she turns her head left, the scene zooms to the left, where some paintings hang on the wall. She moves her head in every direction, trying to learn how to maneuver in her new world. She is anxious to move forward, to see what is beyond the hallway. Her fingers are pressing every button randomly on the other side of the frames. The view changes from a few feet above eye level, then back down to eye level, and then a few steps back. Another button is pressed and the viewer moves a few steps forward. A smile covers Tricia's face, as she continues to press that button to walk through the hallway. As a door opens to the left, she turns her head in that direction and presses the button to enter a room. Another bead of sweat drips down her forehead.

Her senses are now overloaded in this vast room. In the middle is a centerpiece of assorted foods and beverages, where people are mingling. An older woman, glittering in an array of jewelry, is dipping a cracker into a grayish mound in the middle of the centerpiece, exchanging giggles with a young man in a tuxedo. At the other end of the centerpiece are two women drinking champagne, with their drinking arms intertwined. Both are topless. Another man in the corner is putting his glass under a stream of champagne, pouring out from one of the nipples of a statue of RuPaul. In the other corner, a young boy in a double-breasted suit is playing Bach on a grand piano. A dwarf in a tuxedo is maneuvering through the crowd with a tray of flaming hors d'oeuvres. Does anyone see her? She is too nervous to press any buttons, afraid to be seen.

As Tricia moves her head to one side, she sees an aquarium in place of a wall, dark blue but with numerous green-glowing jellyfish gliding very gently upward. As she turns her head to the other side, she again sees no wall but an enormous flat panel display, which is divided into several subsections. In the upper right section is a ticker showing up-to-the-second stock prices. A live shot of the Swiss Alps, with ski conditions listed, is shown in the lower right. From this vantage point, Tricia cannot quite recognize what is displayed on the other sections. As she looks up, a huge portrait is painted on the ceiling, and illuminated from an array of lights pointing to it. Tricia's eyes are now bulging out, and she gasps as she recognizes the portrait. Richie. This must be Richie's house.

The dwarf holding the hors d'oeuvres tray looks directly at her. Her heart is racing as he walks toward her. He is now a few feet away, and she is sweating profusely. What will she say? He quickly passes her. She lets out a sigh of relief, realizing she is invisible. A sly smile forms as she realizes her freedom to explore. She presses a button, but it is the wrong one as she moves backward. Her finger presses the one next to it and she quickly moves forward, across the marble floor. Now in front of the centerpiece, she zeroes in on the goodies. Platters of oysters, clams, caviar, artichoke hearts, shrimp, and those little hot dogs in a blanket all surround a grey mound in the shape of a reclining, curvaceous woman. The mound looks so real; Tricia's curiosity leads her to press the forward button. She is now an arm's length from the mound. She notices crackers in a bowl a few inches from the mound, and sees her own hand reach for a cracker through the glasses. As she is reaching, the mound suddenly sneezes, and in surprise she withdraws her hand from the bowl.

"Richie! I'm glad you could make it!"

Tricia turns her head toward the voice and sees an old man in a suit and tie adjusting his belt. On his belt is an infrared sensor, which flashes a blue dot.

"I can sense you, Richie, but I'm not receiving the visuals.

You still throw the best parties." The old man takes a cracker, and rubs it against the breast portion of the mound, which jiggles a bit but yields some liver pate to the cracker. A bit of flesh is now exposed.

"Richie, I need to tell you something. Can we talk?" The man is now heading out of the room, taking the middle of three long paths.

She is frustrated, as her exploration is cut short for the time being. As she moves forward, she pauses. The room to the left is a dimly lit green, and sports an enormous Jacuzzi with people packed in, drinks in hand, listening to jazz and conversing. As she turns her head to the right, she sees a room with a revolving ice sculpture in the shape of melting timepieces from Dali's "Passage of Time."

"Richie, are you still there?" He is now a few dozen feet in front of her. She accelerates to a few feet from him, and notices his blue light flashes back on. He leads her to an empty red room, a barren shock after her previous sensory stimulation.

"Richie, you've been like a son to me. When I needed to close on Apex Heights, you provided a lending hand. You stood up at my daughter's wedding. God, how I wish it was you she married. Sorry I'm rambling, Richie." The old man now heads outside the room, opening a door that leads to a balcony. His hands are gripped tightly around the railing. Tricia is feeling uncomfortable, sensing the man's uneasiness. She moves toward the balcony.

"Look at the city, Richie, so full of life." He gestures with his hand across the balcony, and thousands of lights can be seen from downtown. His eyes are now tearing, as his voice is choking up. "I'm dying, Richie." The man quickly turns back toward the railing. Tricia's heart is quickly racing. She is deeper into this situation than she cares to be.

"I've given it a lot of thought. I can't take the suffering, dragging my family and myself into a slow death. I must take care of it myself, Richie. You know, I always like to take control." As he turns back toward Tricia, he continues, "You must not tell anyone, not even my family." He moves closer to Tricia and as his belt beeps, he gives her a big hug. She can only see a portion of his shirt and tie, but hears crying. Tricia is shaken up and sweating profusely. She nervously attempts to go backward by pressing a button, but accidentally presses a different button, which puts her into yet another world.

Tricia backs into a door.

The crusted old wooden door flings open and she struggles to regain her balance. She stares ahead at a narrow, decrepit hallway and twenty or so worn and dirty stairs leading up to another floor. The hall smells of urine and blood. Although she is repelled by the sight and stench, Tricia needs to know where she is. Feeding the urge, she continues ahead and up the creaking stairs, being careful not to touch the walls.

Just inside the doorway, Tricia becomes pale. The room she views looks to be an open lobby, very small and dirty. The walls have varicose veins and the paint is old. In the right corner stands a 60-ish man wearing a feathered hat. He smiles and his eyes light as he spots his "guest."

"C'mon in, c'mon in."

Tricia becomes nervous.

"You musta come for da flowers, ta check on da flowers?

TRAZ

Got 'em. Right trew dare." He points toward a long narrow corridor. Beams of dusty daylight sail downward onto the floor of the passageway, as they invite her to continue.

The old man walks from behind a small, green painted desk and walks over in front of Tricia.

"Oh, dats right, dis is your first time in, I never seen ya before, fer sher." He smiles and coughs as he reveals a mouth only half full of teeth.

He coughs again.

"C'mon. Tell Richie I got 'em, jes like I awees do. I got 'em, surely did, got 'em," he mumbles on.

The man leads the way through the corridor.

It looks like a jail, like a prison, maybe the way Alcatraz used to look. She is in a flophouse. In the Bowery. She has the chills.

"I din't know 'im, ya know, Richie's dad. I din't really git what happened. Sad dough, like everyting else ere.

"Git yer clothes on, we got company!" he yells through the open door of the first room on the left. A scared, naked figure reaches for a plush terry robe on a rack screwed to the wall. Tricia momentarily turns away. It really bears no resemblance to a room—it reminds her of a freight elevator, of a jail cell, only not as clean. This five by six-foot room has no carpet; only cracked, broken, grey paint.

It scared her, that chicken wire across the ceiling. A few beer cans lay on top and settled in the middle.

The Room. One small window with bars, one bare bulb for a light. She wishes it were darker; it would be easier to take.

"Dats Tater, he don't like clothes, mosly cus he don't have

163

none, I gis."

Tricia stares straight ahead now, still following. Another room, and the door slams shut, opens, slams shut, opens, slams again.

"Leave it," the man with the feathered hat hollers to his right.

Tricia wants to leave fast. She begins to turn when the man stops. "Wait, look, ya got ta see 'em, nice ones taday."

"Ya know dat Richie . . ."

She stops.

"I likes 'im, we all likes 'im. He gives me all dis money . . . what am I gonna do wit it? I don't need it, got a place right ere. Day don't want it." He points at the room with the naked man. "Where would day go? Day know me, I know dem. I did git a hat dough." He chuckles as his watery eyes light once again.

"Look ere," he points to the large green feather in his already dusty fedora. "I jis hadda git it, always wanted one wit dis fedder." He coughs again. His eyes water. The man with the hat is stopped in front of a closed door. This door has nothing in common with the others. It is made of painted steel. Perfectly painted steel. There is a handle and just above is a card slot. It reminds Tricia of an ordinary hotel room door. Below the handle, however, is a circle of glass, no larger than a nickel.

The man fumbles for what is attached to his belt by a silver chain. He reaches into his pocket and pulls up a plain brown card, inserting and removing it from the slot. He then gently swipes his left hand in front of the glass as his right hand turns the handle.

Tricia's deep green eyes widen and as the man pushes the door open, her mouth gently drops open. On a small circular table is a bouquet of fresh flowers. Blue, red, violet; large and beautiful.

In the far right corner, an easel displays a large photograph of a man in his twenties, in a T-shirt, proudly leaning on an old-style automobile. His eyes squint and his glance looks outward, far past the edge of the picture. The sky is dark behind him.

"Nice huh? I don know what happened butween den an now, but sad ya know. Did e tell ya? Na, don ever will. Look at da flowers dough. Nice."

She nods. And looks.

"Strange . . . like he never did pass . . . look dare."

Directly across the tiny room, on the ivory-painted wall, is a deep burgundy marble stone; rough edges and beautifully carved letters.

She squints through the daylight:

'Dad, I love you'
Renald Harris
1946 -

"He lights da candle sometimes. I know cus I can tell."

Just below is a simple twin-size bed, with a soft-colored sheet—perfectly made. Next to it, a simple stone stand. On top of it, next to the candle, lay a wristwatch, a plain gold wedding band, and an old, creased, wallet-sized picture of a child.

Tricia backs out and walks quickly down the hall toward the stairway. A door slams shut, then opens, and shuts again.

A new button and a new view give Tricia two tones of blue, comprising an endless ocean and sky. She looks left, then right, but the scene does not change character. How does she turn around? She turns her head left as far as she can, but she has not made an about-face. She presses the forward button as she turns her head, and releases the button when her view has made a semicircle. Large colonial homes are scattered on the lush green landscape. Is this a Hawaiian island? She hurries up a winding path, moving her head right, then left, then right as she presses the forward button. As she turns her head left, she moves in front of one of the houses. As she counts the windows and levels of this house, she realizes it is not a house but a mansion. It's a strange mixture of brick and large stone. Roses and geraniums are cascading down from large flowerbeds. The only thing missing is a four-car garage. Above the roof she can see a lighthouse in the background, looking remarkably like the one she scaled many times at Alcatraz.

She now glides forward up the steps to the front of the house. She looks to her left, then to her right. No one around. She has not seen a soul in her new world yet. Now she hears many footsteps, and loud voices. She looks around but still sees no one. Where are these sounds coming from? She quickly rips off the glasses, but still hears the noises. As she looks at her watch, she realizes Richie should be back in half a minute. She jumps off the couch and bolts out of the room, unknowingly leaving Richie's door open.

Obsession

It's now her latest obsession. It consumes her thoughts the entire day. Like a child excited about an upcoming field trip, she was barely able to sleep, and awakens the next morning with butterflies in her stomach. She follows the same routine as the day before, as her watch tells her Richie is about to golf. She is salivating, and quickly heads down his hallway.

As she turns her head in each direction, she attempts to open the door. Ahhhhh! The butterflies in her stomach quickly turn into sinking boulders as she cannot open the door. She turns the knob as if spinning a top, but still no luck. She bends down in front of the doorknob, and notices an infrared sensor staring into her face. Knowing her fingerprint will not get her past this lock; in frustration she gives the door a swift kick. And another. And another.

"Hey, asshole, some people are tryin' to sleep!" a voice in the next unit booms.

She panics, and starts to run down Times Square. She stops by the complaining neighbor's door, gives it one swift Ninja kick, and disappears down the hallway with the speed of a lost particle in an atomic accelerator.

Later that night at a therapy session, Tricia waits for a lull in the discussion.

"How does one go about getting a door lock installed?"

Harold responds, "There's no door locks."

"Weren't you and your boy supposed to install locks on all the doors?"

With fire in his eyes, Harold responds, "First, he's not my

boy. Second, if you find us some hardware for locks, then we'll install them."

"How about some infrared locks? You guys did a nice job on Richie's unit."

"What are you talkin' about?"

"Go try it yourself."

"What are you insinuating?" Spit is dripping out of Harold's mouth.

Tricia firmly states, "If no one else has door locks, he shouldn't either. I demand you remove the lock from his door."

Harold yells, "How did you know there's a lock on his door?"

Another voice shouts, "I know how, she's a snoop, that's how!"

Harold is still yelling. "What other rooms have you been snooping in? If I catch you in my room, your face won't look like your ass anymore!"

All eyes are on her, as the Voice yells, "Hey !@#!!, I bet you're the one that stole my monogrammed underwear."

In the midst of all this, the therapist continues to page through her microbrewery magazine.

Another voice inquires, "Do you know what's in his unit?"

Tricia calmly responds, "Wet bar. Oriental rug. Book shelves. I could go on and on."

Another voice cries, "Hey, he couldn't have snuck that on the island. Who built it for him?"

They all stare at Harold.

Harold says defiantly, "Look. I know you think I did it. No

way in hell would I build anything for that . . ."

Suddenly the bell rings, causing the counselor to flip through the last few pages of her magazine and yell, "Everybody out. Hit the road!!"

Immediately afterwards, Harold hurries over to the 18-year-old's unit.

Bang! Bang! Bang!

But no answer comes from inside the unit.

Bang! Bang! Bang!

"Who the hell is it?" a voice is screaming inside the room.

"Open the damn door!"

"No way. What the hell do ya want?"

"Why did you do it?"

"Do what?"

"Richie's condo."

"What?"

"Wet bar . . . cherry cabinetry . . . book shelves . . . lock . . . does anything ring a bell?"

"That's none of your business. You're not my father."

"Listen, everyone thinks I did it. Well, you're gonna fess up to this, or I'll ring your neck!"

"Kiss the red 'A' on my ass!"

A long period of silence follows. The 18-year-old slowly opens the door, removing the chair propped against the doorknob, and pokes his head out. He looks in both directions of the hallway, but no one is there. With a smirk, he closes the door and props up the chair against it again. He now jumps on his bed, and turns the pages of his dirt bike magazine. Fatigue is setting in, and after a half-hour he is fast asleep.

"Vrrrooooooooooooommm!"

The 18-year-old abruptly awakens and pulls the magazine off his face. Puzzled by the drilling noise from outside his unit, he bolts toward the door. He knocks the chair over as he attempts to open his door, but to no avail. He twists the knob as far as he can, and kicks the door. No luck. He is locked inside his own unit.

"Let me outta here, asshole!"

Autumn

The days grow shorter heading into fall. Goldie and Rhonna notice the sun setting earlier than usual during their evening walks. On one clear, crisp night, they rest on a cliff overlooking the Golden Gate Bridge.

Goldie beams "Look at that postcard—the sun setting over the Golden Gate Bridge."

Rhonna just returns a smile, and brushes her hair back.

Goldie turns toward Rhonna with focused eyes. "Before I was on this island, I never realized this beauty."

Rhonna puts her arm around his waist, and he likewise. They are comfortable with each other, not having to say a word now. As the sun sets, Goldie rests his head on her shoulders. Time seems to move very slowly.

She points up, and whispers to Goldie, "Look, the stars are out tonight."

"That's one advantage of Alcatraz. At least we can see the stars."

"Yep. I know the stars now. But I never paid much attention until we almost lost them."

Goldie now looks up and with a broad stroke of his hand says, "Coca-Cola. Burger King. Tylenol. MasterCard."

Rhonna continues, "At least on Mondays and Wednesdays the stars are out."

"Two days without ads taking over the sky. Big deal."

"What constellation is that?" Rhonna asks as she points up again.

"Don't know. It looks round. The stars seem to go in a circle."

"Maybe it's the new 'A-hole' constellation," Rhonna laughs.

Goldie laughs with her, and they now lie down, face up toward the sky.

Goldie turns to her and points up, "See that star over there?"

"Where?"

"The brightest one up there."

"Oh yeah, that one?"

"Yep. I'm gonna name it 'Rhonna.'"

"Awww. I'm flattered."

He turns toward her to look into her eyes, which now replace the depth and beauty of the evening sky. They embrace.

"Rhonna, I've been taking some walks around the prison. Sometimes, I think you know, I like to just get away from the noise, the complaining, that kind of thing. I've even come across a few special spots, at least what I can imagine to be special on this God-forsaken island. But you know," Goldie's voice becomes quiet, "I've wandered down toward the recreation yard and strayed a little toward the left. I walked into a section of this prison that isn't on the map. There are five or six old cells down there that are what must have been used for solitary confinement. The doors were solid steel. I sneaked a peek in one of them. It was total darkness—no windows, no light. I didn't go inside but I could just imagine. If you ever really want to be alone, this is definitely . . ."

"Let's go . . . show me. Wow, a secret hiding place!" Goldie takes her hand with a smile and leads her to his discovery through a steel gate and down an old corridor. They take a few twists and turns.

"Oh my gosh," Rhonna whispers as they stop in front of a row of six dark steel doors.

"See, no one would even know about this place. You can hear a whisper."

Rhonna moves closer to Goldie as she squeezes his hand. They both softly step toward one of the doors, which is half open.

"Goldie", Rhonna stands on her toes to whisper in his ear. "Let's go inside." Goldie looks at her with a sly smile. "I wanna go inside."

She playfully brushes her body against his and moves her hand up from his back toward his shoulder. Slowly and gently she shifts them both toward the darkness of that cold, empty room.

Knowing Rhonna's intentions as she begins to unbutton his shirt, Goldie softly speaks as she backs him into the cell.

"There are no lights."

"We don't need lights Goldie." She smiles and kisses him passionately.

Goldie reaches toward the door and gently but firmly closes it.

"You didn't lock us in did you, hon?" she giggles as she nibbles his neck.

"Are you scared Rhonna?" Goldie embraces her.

"I've never felt safer, love."

In an embrace of passion, they turn and turn. They dance and sway as they undress each other, their clothes landing on the floor as a blanket to hold them in a sweeter, softer glow, a glow without candles, a glow without light.

Their eyes remain open, yet they cannot see each other, they can only feel the reality of the moment, the heat, the touch, the embrace. All of their other senses seem to take over more than ever before. They hear the breathing of each other's hearts, they share the sweetness of their lips, they smell the scent of each other's breath, and they feel the heat that only the passion of lovers in motion can create in such a cold cell.

Above all, the touch: they turn and play, move down and around the gentle touch of each other's fingertips in this dark steel cabin. The firm caress of each soft curve, the slow swaying of two bodies that have come together for this timeless moment.

There was an irony here that could not escape Goldie. A space once called "the Hole" was, in the past, a blank, empty mortuary designed to isolate a person, built to deprive someone of any and all communication with another human being. It was a dungeon for a solitary being to remain exactly that way; totally isolated in word and thought, let alone touch. It was a dark hell created to leave a man totally alone.

Here though, now, in that same space, with a special person in a special love, it became a place that ended loneliness forever. It became a heaven on earth, where a person shared all he could ever share, everything he is made of, with another— his body, his mind, his soul. One could never become more deeply connected to another, here, in this special place.

They would both come here together often. No one ever found them. No one ever looked.

Thanksgiving

Fall goes by rather quickly. The scribbled and taped wall calendar in the dining hall shows Thanksgiving has arrived. Without family on this Thanksgiving, many islanders are reflective. Some are overcome with a feeling of loneliness, others with a feeling of bitterness. There is a larger showing than usual at Mass.

Arriving a little late for Thanksgiving Mass, Harold walks into the chapel and kneels down. At the end of Mass the priest announces he will hear confessions. As people exit, one man follows the priest into the confessional as Harold waits outside.

The Father welcomes him and says, "You may begin."

The man quickly kneels and excitedly tells the priest, "Father, I have a new service that may help you and all churches across our beautiful country. It may help you save time from the many confessions you hear, and make confessing as easy as picking up a phone. It works like this: a parishioner picks up the phone and dials 1-900-CONFESS, and an announcement tells him or her to enter the number of the commandment that was violated. After this is entered, the caller is told to enter how many times the commandment was violated, and the user presses this number in. This menu can be repeated many times, so many commandments can be entered."

The priest in anger exclaims, "Next, please."

The man stands up and says, "If you change your . . ." at which point he is interrupted again by the priest exclaiming, "Next!"

Soon Harold is the only one left as he heads into the confessional. He tells the priest, "Father, as strange as it sounds, I'm not here to confess. I just need to get a few things off my chest."

The priest responds, "I understand, please continue."

"I worked hard, provided for my family, believed in God—where has it gotten me? I've been trapped here with all these assholes—pardon the language, Father."

"I'm not here to judge," the priest says.

"But Father, I've always leveled with people—told them the truth. Maybe I was too coarse in doing so. But you know, Father, people are just too sensitive nowadays. You can't say anything to anyone without them getting offended. Maybe I was too rough on the ones I love, but Father, I'll never understand how they could turn me in. I mean my own wife. She should be grateful to me, yet she turned me in. She's the one that forced me to live in this homo town. Father, I think about 90% of the people in San Francisco must be gay. I was afraid to eat at restaurants for fear of catching AIDS. I sacrificed for her and where did that get me—now I'm on Homo Island. My God, it hurts, but I still love my kid, how I miss my kid. I wrote him letters but never got any back. What do I do?"

"First, get rid of your hatred. Show compassion for people different than yourself. They are your brothers too. When you get off the island, tell your family that you love them. Learn from your mistakes, and try in good faith not to repeat them. In your heart realize that above all, love is the answer."

"But Father . . ."

"I know that confession should be anonymous, but I want to thank you now for building this confessional and pews. You're quite a handyman."

"Thank you, Father."

As Harold leaves the church, he begins to reflect, and a feeling of peacefulness follows him to his condo unit. His confession relieved some of his burden. He now feels he can show more compassion. When Harold enters his room, he glances at the picture of a little league team huddled together. He sees himself smiling, standing in the center of the children. It brings back warm memories of the winning season, and what a complete feeling of joy it was to win the championship.

He then picks up his baseball and glove, and gently tosses the ball into the air.

He remembers the crowd cheering after they won the big game, and him being so proud of his son Donny, who hugged him so hard.

POOF! Harold tosses the ball into his glove.

But that winning season was two years ago. How things change.

WHOOSH! He tosses the ball into his glove again.

His wife said not to push his son too hard, but to let him have a variety of interests. After all, she said, it's only a game. But these other interests got in the way. School work. Jewelry making . . .

THWACK!! He pounds the ball into his mitt.

He let his wife have her way, but his son started to lose focus, lose ability. And his son would miss a practice here and there. And the team started to lose.

SLAM!!! The ball's velocity rips the seam of the mitt.

She is turning his son into a loser, a sissy.

BAMM!!! His condo wall now has a dent the size of a baseball. Harold tosses the glove into the air, and retires his game of pitch and catch for the day.

Later that day, Rhonna is pleading in the hallway, "My mom. I have to call her. It's been . . . please can I use your phone?"

But an old man just responds with a puzzled look.

Rhonna continues, "Someone in the next hallway said you have a phone—please may I?"

At this point a tall, tanned man in a silk and cotton sweater is walking by, and momentarily stops near the two.

The old man yells back at Rhonna, "A phone? I don't know what in the hell you're talking about." He walks a few paces into his condo unit and slams the door. As tears are welling up in Rhonna's eyes, the tanned man approaches her.

"I couldn't help but overhear."

But Rhonna's head is hung as she starts to walk away.

He continues, "You indicated you need a phone. I think I can help."

Rhonna stops and wipes her eyes. Sounding a bit suspicious, she mutters, "How?"

"My condo is the last unit on the left. Stop by anytime."

"You have a phone?"

He nods with a smile.

Her face suddenly lightens up. "I don't want to interrupt your dinner; it'll be served in a little while. How about after dinner?"

"See you then. By the way, my friends call me "Richie." What's your name?"

"Rhonna."

"What a pleasant name. Oh, Rhonna, please don't tell anyone about the phone."

"You have my word."

In line for Thanksgiving dinner later that afternoon, some islanders complain, "Where the hell is the turkey?"

Another joins in, "How about the stuffing and sweet potatoes?"

Another yells, "Where the hell is the duck blood soup?"

But ham and eggs are served instead of turkey, with a unique blend of spices. When everyone sits down with his or her plate, the 18-year-old stands up, clears his throat, and looks toward the Cajun chef, who is replacing an empty tray with a full one. He proceeds to recite his most recent work:

I do not like Cajun eggs and ham
I do not like them Sam-I-Am

I do not want my gut to hurt
I do not want my shit to squirt

I do not like explosive gas
I do not like blood outta my ass

I do not want my piss to smoke
I do not like your sick, sick joke.

The Cajun chef ignores the young man, and hurries into the kitchen. As the young man sits down, many at his table are giving him an ovation. Most of the others, however, are ignoring him.

As Tricia sits down at a busy table, the people on each side of her immediately get up and leave. Unfazed, she settles in for her holiday meal. As she is about to take her first bite of ham, the Cub fan takes a seat next to her.

"Looks like we're stuck in the bleacher section today!" he chuckles as he places his tray down.

She politely smiles as she notices his blue pinstriped jersey. Someone yells from another table "Hey Santo, are you gonna make a play for her?" Another laughs "Let me know when you make it to first base!"

Ignoring them, the Cub fan remarks to Tricia "Did you ever sit in the bleachers at the Friendly Confines?"

"What?"

"The bleachers at Wrigley field. You know, the home of the Chicago Cubs."

"Oh, no, I haven't," she replies dispassionately.

"Have I got a story for you! Way back in '83, well, you probably were a twinkle in your mom's eye, I was sittin' in the bleachers for the Cubs-Cardinals game. Bruce Sutter was on the mound, the ex-Cub traded to the Cards. Boy, could he throw that split-fingered fastball. I never seen a ball sink like that near home plate."

She is oblivious to the story, and instead is holding up a piece of ham as if under investigation.

The Cub fan continues, "Up steps Ryno to the plate in extra innings. Well, I don't need to tell you what happened next. The second I heard the crack of the bat, I knew the ball was gone. Us bleacher bums all jumped up, and the ball was headin' my way. My heart must have been jumpin' out of my chest. I bent over to grab my mitt." The Cub fan now reenacts the moment with hand gestures.

"I then saw it sailing to the right of me." The fan now swings his right arm wildly, and knocks over a gravy bowl right in front of Tricia. The bowl tumbles over and the gravy splashes on Tricia's hands.

She bolts up and shakes her hands.

"Crap! You idiot! Look at what you . . ."

Déjà vu . . .

"Oh, I'm so sorry, let me help you with that." He looks around for napkins. Unable to find any, he takes off his jersey and starts to wipe Tricia's hands with it.

"Ah! Get away from me." She feels the sting of the Cajun's spices, and as she is about to scream she notices that the red ink on her hands has magically disappeared. As if she has witnessed a miracle, she raises her hands upward and looks at them in astonishment.

The Cub fan stares at his jersey, and is puzzled as to why the colors are fading.

While the other islanders continue eating, an uncomfortable silence settles in.

The mood at dinner becomes rather reflective. One islander with speckled glasses turns toward another and lets out a sigh as he puts his coffee mug down. "We're blowing a perfect opportunity. We could have a possible utopia right in our hands."

The other islander laughs as he questions, "What are you talking about?"

"Everyone in America is sick and tired of the crime rate, the poverty, racism, dirty politicians—you name it." He picks up his mug to take another drink.

The man next to him says, "So?"

He lets out another sigh as he says, "Well, we have a chance here to start from scratch, to make up our own rules, rules that really make sense. We have just the right amount of people to form a real community, not like in America where millions live by each other in one impersonal mass."

The other man replies with a grin, "There's only one problem with your scenario."

The bespeckled man halts applying his mug to his mouth as he says, "What's that?"

"There's only A-holes here."

After dinner, Tricia sneaks into the quiet kitchen. She quickly opens up all the cabinet doors, and then the fridge. Her eyes light up as she spots the vat of gravy. She gives herself a sponge bath in the kitchen sink, rubbing her arms and legs while holding back the tears.

Also, immediately after dinner, Rhonna walks through Times Square. She looks over her shoulder and notices the prisoners are nowhere in sight. All are out in recreation areas or involved in daily tasks. She knocks quietly on Richie's door. The door slowly opens and Rhonna smiles instantly. It is a genuine smile, a smile of joy coupled with thanks.

"Come in," says Richie, dressed comfortably, his smile complements the details of his clothing. Rhonna greets him with a hug, stares in his eyes, and shakes from side to side. She notices his "cell" is actually a "suite."

"Is this your cell, Richie? You've sure got it all."

"Friends share, don't they?" he replies. "How about a holiday drink?", he asks as he gently strolls into a closet containing a wide assortment of bottles. "May I suggest a '67 or '68 Cabernet Sauvignon, or maybe a '67 Sherry?"

"OK, and put that inside of a gift-wrapped, baby-blue, '57 Chevy and I'll take it!" she laughs. "You know, for the first time this season, the holiday spirit has hit me."

"I think it will get better, Rhonna. Come here," he says as he pours the wine in both glasses. "You need to make a phone call, right?"

"Shall I call now?" she asks impatiently, yet politely.

"If you like. Here, follow me. Oh, um." He turns around and looks as if he is concerned.

"What is it? Can't I get a hold of . . ."

"Ha, ha," he chuckles as he points to the sofa and sits down. He taps the sofa as if he wants her to sit next to him. She does.

"Rhonna, you wanted to be close to someone this Thanksgiving, and I want you to . . . to be closer than just a phone call."

She seems puzzled as she stares at him while sipping her wine. Her eyes never leave his, at least not as he explains.

"There is something about you, Rhonna. I think it is something that I lack. I always tried to make the holidays special, but never did I make such a simple gesture that could really change the way people feel, at least until now. Look at that monitor, Rhonna." Richie points his hand toward a wall, where a large grey area suddenly lights; then seems to paint a picture of a place Rhonna knows.

"Oh, Rich; it can't be, it just can't be my . . . Richie, it's my home, my mama's house! Look! There's the china cabinet, and oh, the shelf with all my stuffed animals. Oh, how did you . . ."

Suddenly, in the corner of the screen, a small grey square appears and an older woman's face slowly materializes within it. The face is smiling, and a tear falls upon a creviced cheek.

"Oh, Mother, it's you!" Rhonna turns her head toward Richie and flashes back to the screen.

"You did it, Richie, how did you . . . ?" She breaks into a tearful cry of joy. "It's me. Dear God, I prayed for this day."

"Oh, mother, how I've missed you!" Her eyes are filled with tears. "Dammit! You're so far away—too far!" Her eyes never leave the screen.

"I know dear, but . . ." As Rhonna's mother is talking, her image slowly breaks out of the small square boundaries and into the large screen area of her home. She is now seen standing with her arms outstretched as if she is waiting to hold something.

"What is it, Mom, you need something, what is it?" Rhonna asks in a concerned tone. "Are you OK?"

Rhonna glances at Richie.

"Yes, she's OK. Here," Richie smiles as he hands his glasses to her, "put these on."

Rhonna has seen something like this before. She places the glasses over her eyes.

"OK, Mrs. Kinsey, put them on."

"We're set."

Richie punches in a few keys and explains, "Rhonna, you can go home." Richie is choked up as he chuckles, much like Scrooge on Christmas morning.

"Go ahead and take a walk with your mother."

Rhonna stands up, facing the screen. She enters a virtual world where there are no dimensional boundaries. Her mother's form becomes real; she is in her mother's house. They embrace. Richie smiles as he quietly gets up to leave the room. He senses the privacy of a mother-daughter visit.

Rhonna doesn't notice he left. She glances around the room she's in, her mom's living room. There is one well-worn reclining chair next to an end table, on which an open book rests. As Rhonna gazes at the knick-knacks on the coffee table, she notices a youthful portrait of her mom, smiling, holding a young, giggling girl on her lap. Has it been that many years since her age of innocence? As she turns her head toward the adjacent room, the dining room, she sees a place setting on the dining room table; one plate, one fork, one knife, and one empty glass.

As they are now holding each other's hands, Rhonna notices for the first time how worn and wrinkled her mom's hands have become. She senses a vulnerability and loneliness in her mom for the first time.

"As soon as I'm out, I'll be over, Mother. There's so much

we need to catch up on."

"Dear, I wish it could be now. I've written to the mayor, the governor, even the President about your unfair situation. I would do anything to help. Please let me know what I can do."

"Mom, just take care of yourself. Be there for me when I get back."

At this, Rhonna turns away from her mother, whose eyes have been fixed on her the entire time. She puts her hands over her special glasses, and begins to weep.

"It's OK, dear," her mother walks toward her and takes Rhonna's head to her shoulder. She strokes her long blonde hair.

"Mother." Rhonna lifts her head as her eyes suddenly squint within the puzzled frame of her face. She pulls her head away from her mother, a questioning look in her eyes. The signs suddenly seem to have taken hold of Rhonna and shaken her. Her tears disappear into a look of concern.

She walks back suddenly—five steps.

"Mother, walk toward me."

"Dear, listen . . ."

"Do it, Mom, please."

A limp is detected as Rhonna feels a cool wash of reality run through her veins.

"You're limping. Mom, talk, say something!"

Her mother makes every effort to say exactly what she means, without hesitation . . . but in a slow, imprecise, unconvincing way, the words slip out.

"Dear, you need to know that I am all right."

Rhonna listens as a slur taints her words of assurance. She shakes her head.

"No!" Tears again begin to fill her eyes.

"You need someone with you!"

Rhonna realizes the near impossible remedy to the situation.

There is no one else.

Rhonna quickly moves toward her suddenly fragile mother and assists her to the recliner. They both sit down to talk.

Richie now re-enters the room, only to quietly make his way out of the condo. He hears Rhonna's voice as he glances back to see two grey shadows, hovering together against the backdrop of his prison wall. He overhears Rhonna say, "No one can keep me here!" Her determination reminds him of himself. He thinks back to when he was a child. He becomes that child again for the next hour, remembering the details as he had not done in a long, long time. As he left home, the tears his mother had shed found no place in Richie. The courage of a child without a father could make one so strong he could almost grow cold. It is as though you need to become . . . well, Richie didn't think that far into the present. He heads back to the condo.

He returns to find Rhonna alone, staring at the now stark white wall where her mother lived. His entrance awakens her and she turns.

"Richie."

"What is it?" he notices her tremble.

"Don't speak, there is something wrong. She had a stroke."

Ansell Roberts

She gets up to leave, but collapses in his arms. Richie stares solemnly ahead as he comforts her.

>*Nothing, no one to hold*
>*it is all here, but not . . .*
>*not in the same sense,*
>*the tangible sense,*
>*I've forgotten what it*
>*is like*
>*to feel this . . .*
>>>*this being*
>*this hand, this object*
>*this love, this life*

Richie has not comforted someone in such a long time. He can't recall a time he gave a gift to someone else in a form so unfamiliar.

"I can't wait, I just can't wait," she softly speaks. "I need to be there for her."

The two hold onto each other.

He replies softly, "Rhonna, we will meet again and talk . . . there will be a signal."

"A signal—what do you mean?"

"We'll meet again. When the time is right, I'll get you out of here."

"When?"

"When the time is right. Please do not tell anyone about today, as it must be our secret."

"But . . ."

"No one else must know."

"No one?"

"No."

After a long period of silence, Rhonna thanks Richie and quietly exits the room, tears in her eyes.

Rainy Day

The rains arrive with winter. The bulbous plants on the island, including tulips, gladiolus, and daffodils, first bloom in this rainy season. Other plants, such as geraniums and roses, join the kaleidoscope of color. For the caretakers, this is an advantage. But for other islanders, the rain means more time to spend inside the cell house with each other. For Goldie and Rhonna, their walks are initially hampered.

One morning Goldie walks through Broadway on his way to Rhonna's unit. He passes the Voice, who is pounding on Tricia's door.

"Why the !$@!! didn't you order us raincoats or umbrellas?"

Tricia yells back, "I only accept food orders."

"Listen, I slipped a note under your door last week. You never got back to me!"

"Want me to repeat it in another language? How about imbecilis?"

The pounding on the door is louder. "You order that hot $@!! sauce for dinner, but you can't order stuff we need?"

"I don't order the hot sauce . . ."

Goldie grins as he turns the corner. He taps on Rhonna's door, which immediately opens.

"Goldie, where did you get that?" She smiles as she notices a plastic sheet, like a poncho, draped over his head and around his body.

"Just some unused garbage liners from the laundry room. Got one for you too," he says as he holds up another liner.

She giggles, "How hard is it raining today?"

"Just a drizzle. Here, let's slip this over your head." As she tries to put it over her, the opening for the head is too small. He pulls out a pair of scissors and cuts through the liner a bit more.

"Here, this should fit perfectly."

She tries it again and says, "How do I look?"

"Simply mahveloussss!"

"Where should we go?"

"Let's head down the paved path to the sally port. There's a room with a scenic view there. The other paths will be muddy, especially the Agave Trail."

As they head down the path, Rhonna says dejectedly, "Christmas is only a few weeks away. This is the first time it doesn't feel like Christmas."

"Yeah . . ."

She looks downward, and her expression changes several times, as if she is replaying a scene in her head.

"This is so unfair. They didn't just punish us. They punished our families, also." After a moment of hesitation she continues, "How did you used to spend Christmas?"

"Unfortunately, I was always moving from place to place. I spent many a Christmas alone. As far as Christmas meals go, White Castle was one of them."

Rhonna looks at him sadly, yet in his heart he feels that this may be his best Christmas, to be able to spend it with someone he loves.

As they near the sally port, Rhonna says, "Do you mind if we turn back?"

"Is everything OK?"

"Yeah, I guess the rain's getting me down."

After a few minutes back up the trail, Goldie interjects in the silence, "The others. They seem like zombies in the dining hall lately."

"It seems to be getting quieter as Christmas approaches." She now sweeps her arm in panoramic style. "Look around the island. No lights, no decorations. No way to tell this is the holiday season."

"No music. I used to think Christmas tunes were corny. But I miss the holiday music and those old Christmas movies."

He now puts his hand into hers as they enter the cell house.

Later that day, Rhonna swings open her door as she heads to the dining hall for dinner. She reaches back to shut the door, and is startled by something hanging on it—a giant wreath, with ivy spun around a circle of scrap metal, and roses spread around the ivy. The wreath is still dripping wet. Christmas reds and greens now decorate this colorless hallway. With a sudden feeling of lightness, she turns down the aisle and heads toward Goldie's condo.

Cleansing of the Soul

It is early morning, dark, before sunrise. A woman in her late 20's knocks on a door. As the man answers the door, the woman stutters a bit as she says, "Um, excuse me, can I come in?"

The man says without hesitation, "Certainly." The woman follows him inside his condo to a simple table with two chairs. The table and chairs are old and wooden, but in good shape. His entire condo is simple, more so than the others. He turns on a lamp on the way to the table. On the same table as the lamp is a small Nativity scene, which is dimly lit, but warm.

The man says politely, "Please, sit down."

The woman forces a momentary smile of politeness as she responds, "Thank you. I hope I didn't wake you up."

"Oh, no. I am up this early quite often! I'm an early riser!" He looks at her with a smile that tells her it's OK, not an inconvenience. "How can I help you?"

"I don't know if you know me, Father, if you've seen me around. My name is . . ."

"Yes, I have seen you before. Hello, I'm Father James." He extends his hand and smiles.

"I couldn't sleep. I probably look it, huh?" She glances down at the table and then looks back up at the priest. Her arms are crossed between her legs as she sits. She appears cold. "There's something that's been bothering me; sometimes it even keeps me awake, like last night." She stops talking for a moment, her eyes staring downward.

"Please go on."

"I just lay awake and think . . ." She pauses and looks up at the priest. "It's hard for me to tell you this. About a year ago . . . I made the decision to have an abortion." Her speech nervously accelerates. "It wasn't a rash decision. I thought about it . . . a lot. I thought—is it right, is it wrong? I know how you feel about it, Father, how the church feels. But for me it wasn't like that. There was no clear-cut line in my head. How wrong could it be? It's my body, right? Why should I let someone else tell me what to do with it? It's just a fetus. It can't survive on its own. How could it be a life? I knew of countless women who had them, abortions I mean, and they seemed unaffected by it. It seemed to work for them, and these are intelligent women!"

"I know what you mean. I've spoken to these women myself. Most of them seem rather convinced that what they do with their bodies is their personal affair, that our hand should not be in it, that our pro-life beliefs are not valid."

"Yes, I know."

"Tell me, did you seek counseling prior to your decision?"

"Oh sure, I got counseling from my friends, family, and doctor." She motions as if she is the doctor handing out an abortion pill. "Oh yeah, I got advice from my husband," she says sarcastically and laughs. "Oh yes, and I went to family planning. They pretty much left it up to me. They said *when* I decided to go ahead with it, here's the address."

"The ring on your finger, I take it you are or were married? What did your husband say? Did he help at all?"

"He helped. He helped me remember that when we became engaged, we agreed that a family, kids, were not in our immediate plan. That was down the road. I had my career and he had goals that didn't involve a child. He said he was a professional, climbing the ladder, with no time for kids. He'd be busy 24 hours a day, work, school . . . That was part of the reason I decided to go ahead with it. I mean, without support from your husband, your sleepless nights with a baby aren't going to get any easier." She pauses, and continues more slowly, her eyes staring downward. "As it turns out—my sleepless nights without a baby—I don't think that will ever become easier. But I'm not blaming him, Father. It was my decision. When it comes down to it, it was all mine."

"So from your husband's standpoint, aborting the child was the thing to do?"

"It seemed that way to me."

"What you are describing here are all of these outside forces and opinions that so often, in so many ways, seem to shape our thinking, our own decision-making. It is rare we get a chance, or take the time, the real alone time, to make such a decision—based purely on our own beliefs, our own morals, what is really the right or wrong thing to do. Is it this decision to get the abortion that keeps you awake, like last night?"

"Yes, it is. Since I've gone through with it, it's like I can't forget it. I was a mess the first day and for a while after. I think I was in shock. I'm past that now, but I just keep thinking . . ."

She starts to drift off. "You know, as a girl, I always wanted a baby." She starts to smile sadly.

"Oh, yes! The dream of every little girl!"

"I know. And guess what? That dream never really left me. I really wanted a child. I guess it seemed the timing wasn't just right. You know, some couples wait to buy a home, make a move. And some just wait to have a family. I guess I finally thought it best just to wait. But that wasn't right, it wasn't the right way to do it." Her voice and demeanor become firm. "I shouldn't have had . . . My friends were wrong, my husband was wrong, I was wrong. That was a child. I know that now; I've seen things, you know. I've since seen a video of a child inside the womb! That is not just a fetus, it is a life! This video showed a fetus just a few months old. It had fingers, toes, eyes, and a nose. It was moving around. That baby had a personality! I thought God, that is a life! Now why in the hell didn't the people at the family planning center show me this, even a picture, anything? What . . . maybe I would have thought more . . ."

"My dear, we are living in a world where any life that is not viable is not a human life. It is the same with the elderly."

"It's terrible, Father, just terrible. And I'm terrible, just a part of it. I took my child's life."

She breaks down. The priest reaches across the table and takes her hands.

"I see that you are suffering. I understand. God understands and God forgives."

"I want to confess this, Father." She looks up as her crying subsides. "Please forgive me."

"You are forgiven. I hereby absolve you of all your sins."

He makes the sign of the cross in front of her. His other hand is still holding hers. Tears begin to well in his eyes. "You have gone through a terrible time with a lot of guilt. It is part of the post-traumatic stress syndrome. It is okay to grieve for the loss of a loved one. Please don't be afraid to cry."

As she tries to compose herself, she says, "You know, there are times when I see a child, about a year old, and think to myself, my child would have been that age. And I just look, and think . . . what would my baby be like? Some months ago, I was at an amusement park with my husband, just looking at this large Ferris wheel all lit up, when I caught a glimpse of a couple and their son. He was a cute blonde boy and I found myself just staring at him. I looked at the wonder in his big blue eyes as he took all this in, this enormous wheel of lights. I just watched the way he moved and laughed. I listened to his voice . . . just stood there staring and wondering if my baby was a boy, would he look that way? What a wonderful new world this would have been for him. Well, finally his father looked over and noticed me. I don't know what he must have thought. I know now I will never go through with that again. I will never deny a life and all that goes with it."

"I know that."

"Thank you for listening, Father." She squeezes his hands in a grateful manner and manages a smile. The look on her face reveals a great load has been lightened.

"That is not necessary, thank our Lord. You are still young and you've learned a lot through this. There will be another chance for you, I promise." He looks at her with a smile and pats her hand.

"Thank you." She pauses and looks at the priest. "You know,

you just reminded . . . I can't help remembering that there was a priest nearby, at that abortion clinic. This is terrible—he was standing there on the sidewalk about half a block away from the entrance. He was talking to a passerby, not yelling or threatening, or anything like that, just talking. He was handing out some leaflets, probably some pro-life literature or something of that nature, to couples or just anyone who walked by.

"Well, walking in front of me was a young girl, obviously on her way into the clinic. The priest tried to talk to her as she passed his way. I saw him say something—he seemed friendly enough—he was smiling while he was talking. She stopped and listened for a second, and then he tried to give her a piece of paper. She all of a sudden started yelling at him, calling him an asshole and the whole nine yards. He just stood there.

"The next thing I see is a car speed by me and pull up by the curb next to them. This young guy jumps out—it must have been her boyfriend or husband, or whatever—and just starts laying into him while the girl stands there watching. The guy is yelling, cursing at the priest while he's just standing there and taking it. Pretty soon there are other people watching, too. I just froze, you know, kind of backed off and kept my distance. Then the guy grabs the papers from the priest's hands and flings them all over the place, and he's still yelling! Then he starts shoving the priest, calling him every name in the book. Well, he finally falls backwards, yeah, the guy knocked the priest to the ground. He looks down at him and yells to his girlfriend to go ahead and go in, then hops back in his car. She turns to look at the priest who is trying to pick up these papers and calls him an asshole! No one who was watching helped him up, helped him pick up his papers. Someone even joined in to call him an asshole. I felt sorry for him."

"Those papers were handouts. They contained a chapter from the Bible—Luke, chapter one, from the New Testament. I know. That priest was me."

"It was you?"

"Yes, I chose that particular chapter because of what it says so simply about birth, about conception, and about the soul of a child in the womb. It is about Jesus, the Angel Gabriel announcing to Mary that she will be the Mother of God. It was God's plan for her. Luke also describes God's plan that Mary's relative gives birth to a son, John the Baptist. Gabriel announced to Elizabeth's husband that he would have a son, that he would be great in the eyes of the Lord.

You see, God's plan was made even before his child's conception. And when Mary went to visit Elizabeth when she was six months pregnant, John, still in her womb, leapt for joy when Elizabeth heard Mary's greeting. They both knew of Mary's blessing, that she would become the Mother of Our Lord, that Jesus would be born to her."

While the priest describes this gospel, the woman is contemplating the Nativity scene, which has a soft, glowing look. The priest continues, "A fellow priest used this gospel a long time ago, to help the people of his parish understand that each child is given a soul, that God has a plan for every child, even when he is in his mother's womb; yes, even before he is conceived. It is right to let God's plan be fulfilled.

"His message came across so clear that day, that I thought I might use this to help change the minds of some people considering abortion, or at the very least give them something to consider beforehand. I have been doing this for a long time, staying within certain boundaries, just talking, trying to give people this written message. You know that day you saw me, that kind of reaction wasn't that unusual. I've hit the ground before. But I do it because if I can change one mind, it is worthwhile."

"I don't know what to say now. Well, what you do is good, Father. It's right. It's selfless, too. And to be treated like that for pure goodness, I just don't know. There is no justice. I mean, when I think of some of the things I've done, someone could have shoved me around and I'd have deserved it. I'm a real as . . . I belong here."

"Don't say that about yourself. We all have done things we regret. But we always learn from them."

"But I'm glad you're here, Father, although I don't know why you would ever choose a God-forsaken—excuse my expression—place like this to carry out your mission. Well, on second thought, we could use the Word of the Lord here probably as much as anywhere else."

"Yes, it worked out well for me, I think. Although I must tell you that I did not choose to work here, even though it is very fulfilling. I was sent here, as you were. It seems I was thought of as a lawbreaker one too many times for the work I was doing near the abortion clinics. But my work is here for right now, and that must be God's will. You know, I followed every rule by the law, always kept my space, distance. But it seems that . . . well, I'm here now and that is God's plan for me. I will not second-guess it."

Christmas Eve

Christmas Eve dinner. Nothing to separate it from other meals. Nothing on the island even suggests a hint of Christmas, except a small wreath hanging on a colorless condo door.

As the islanders line up for their grub, they notice the food trays are empty.

"Where the hell is the food?" voices echo.

A voice from the kitchen hollers, "Jest a min!"

"Shake your ass!" the Voice yells.

Some are sitting down at the tables, with empty plates and table settings in front of them. An old man pulls out his wallet as he softly says to the person next to him, "Want to see pictures of what I'm missing this Christmas?" He turns to the images of three smiling children, apparently his grandkids, and takes the picture out of his wallet.

The person next to him takes his fork and pokes it through the three smiling kids, as he yells back, "They look like spoiled brats."

The old man is now visibly shaking, and leaves the dining room.

At another table, a frail woman is asking, "Hey, has anyone gotten any mail recently? I shoulda got some Christmas cards from my family, but nothing came."

Another woman at the same table complains, "Even in jail they get decorations for their cells. You would think they would give us each a wreath."

The frail lady responds, "Maybe we didn't get the wreaths because they sent them by mail."

The islanders are now edgy and are banging on the tables with their forks and knives, hooting and hollering. While the Cajun chef is nervously preparing the meal, he accidentally drops an open jar of Cajun sauce in the turkey gravy. He quickly scoops it up with his ladle, and sticks his finger in the ladle. He licks his finger and exclaims, "Ooh, mama on the bayou, you is still an insporation!" After carving up the turkey and pouring on the gravy, the chef bursts from the kitchen with a big "Ayooo! Mare-y Crissmoss!" welcome.

At a table close to the kitchen door, one man yells to another, "Hey, you should bathe once in a while—your BO could kill a skunk."

The other man responds, "Then move yer ass somewhere else."

"Screw you, this is my table!"

The other man belches in the first man's face.

At another table, the Voice is yelling with turkey in his mouth, "Sobitch! Sobitch!" as he quickly guzzles some water. A blood-curdling scream is heard at another table.

A man in overalls stands up and shouts toward the kitchen, "You call this shit a Christmas meal? Hot pepper on turkey?"

He turns over his tray and yells, "I got peppers comin' out of my ass the last few weeks!"

Harold joins in and yells, "I can't feel my tongue!" as he throws his turkey at the kitchen door, his veggies at one table, and flings his potato salad at another table.

"Strike!" yells Big Boy as the potato salad hits the buttocks of a woman bending down. She slips and falls over, dragging people down as she struggles to get up. Big Boy then takes off his shirt, and starts towel whipping those at this table shouting, "Yeee Haaaaa!".

Others are clutching their throats, battling for the remaining pitchers of water. At one table, an elderly man grabs the pitcher and pulls it toward his lips. Before it touches his lips, a massive hairy arm decorated in camouflage grabs him from behind. The other arm presses a Bowie knife against his Adam's apple, as it quivers up and down. "Put the pitcher back on the table. Now! Spill a drop and I'll carve you like a Christmas goose!"

At another table a man coughs his food into his neighbor's face. The recipient of the cough cups his hands to his eyes, screaming "My eyes, my eyes, I can't see!" He leaps up in a panic and stumbles into others as he tries to run toward the exit. "Medic, Medic!"

Others are throwing their forks and knives in the direction of the kitchen.

"Oww, I'm hit," screams another as he pulls a fork from his leg.

Now plates, forks, and knives are being launched in all directions. The sounds of broken porcelain echo throughout the dining hall.

The 18-year-old climbs up the bars of the dining hall to gain a vantage point. He reaches into a sack of smoking hot turkey legs with one hand, while holding onto the bar with the other. His first target is Harold. The first heat-seeking missile strikes Harold from behind, with follow-up strikes.

"What the hell?" Harold screams as he is disoriented. "My legs are on fire!"

The next victim is Tricia, as a missile hits her hairdo. She cries "What the?" as she frantically struggles to find the turkey bone in her hair. The 18-year-old now targets random victims.

The red-haired man turns over the whole table and throws his cup and plate against the wall.

Through all of this, there is one man left sitting at a table, oblivious to the riot. He is pouring sweat, yet calmly enjoying his Christmas meal. He has built up an immunity to the chef's cooking, and actually savors it.

The man in overalls yells toward the kitchen, "I'm goin' ta shove this jalapeno pepper up your ass!" He runs screaming toward the kitchen, clutching a jalapeno pepper. The chef, fearing his life's possessions will be destroyed, grabs a few of his sacred spices from the kitchen shelf. As he hurries toward the door with bottles labeled "Ass in the Tub," "Nuclear Hell," "Bad Girls in Heat," and "Mo Hotta Mo Betta," the kitchen door swings open. The man in overalls bursts in, chasing the chef around the kitchen table and out the kitchen door.

"Aaaeeee!!!" the chef cries out as he hurries out of the dining hall. Now Harold and the red-haired man join the man in overalls in hot pursuit of the chef. The chef heads into the hallway and down the stairs, with his bottles jingling as they hit against each other. The caps have loosened on a few of his bottles and as he bounces down the stairs, sauce pours onto the steps. As the chef reaches the basement, the man in overalls, Harold, and the red-haired man are the first ones to reach the stairs. In a few seconds they let out a cry.

"Ah, shit!!!"

"What the hell?"

They are now piled on top of each other as they have slipped on the Cajun sauce.

"My Goddamn foot!"

"Ahhh!! What's eatin' through my pants?"

In a panic, the chef quickly scans the basement for a place to hide. Nothing but cement walls to the right and straight-ahead. To the left is a door labeled "KEEP OUT," toward which the chef quickly scampers. First turning and then yanking on the doorknob with no success, the pale chef now nervously looks back. His pursuers, still moaning and groaning, have not made it down the stairs yet. Looking toward the stairs, he notices his sauce has spilled. His eyes now follow the sauce from the stairs to the tops of his shoes. Sweat is pouring down his forehead as he realizes he left a bloody trail. He rearranges his bottles in an upright position, while his wide eyes nervously bounce around the room. No other place to hide. Gently, he tiptoes toward the stairway and crouches down underneath it.

Just in time. Through the large crack in the crooked stairs, the chef sees the backs of his pursuers' shoes as they hurry down the stairs. As they look around, the man in overalls angrily says, "Where the hell is that mutha fucka?"

Harold, pointing toward the floor, says, "Follow that trail!"

The red-haired man hurries, Harold hobbles, and the man in overalls hops toward the door. Unable to open it, the red-haired head man lets out a few expletives. Harold immediately rushes the door, his protruding stomach making first contact with old wood. The door gives way, and a loud groan is heard from Harold as he barrels inside the room. The red-haired man and the man in overalls quickly enter the room.

The chef hears voices from inside the room.

"We're gonna string you up, you bastard!"

"He must be hiding behind one of these barrels!"

Some of the bottles are nervously rattling against each other in the chef's shaking hands. A loud thud echoes from inside the room, and a barrel rolls through the door. The chef moves his sweating head out from behind the stairs in time to see the large wooden barrel roll into the cement wall and then roll back again. He listens intently to the voices from inside the room.

"Wait. What's in these barrels?"

"I don't know, but the room smells like beer."

"Yep, this barrel reeks of beer."

Another loud thud.

"Is it empty?"

"Damn. There's gotta be one with beer in it."

Several loud thuds. Another barrel rolls out of the room. Then another. Then another.

"Damnit!"

"Not one! Not one!"

"Who drank all the damn beer?"

As the red-haired man and his partners emerge from the room, the chef quickly moves his head back under the stairs.

The red-haired man swiftly kicks a barrel, and his foots breaks through the wood, causing wood splinters to fly across the room. Harold bends over and reads writing scribbled across one of the barrels.

"Room 314, Barracks Road. Must be on the third story of the barracks building. Who lives there?"

"I don't know. Look, this one's also got that address on it."

"Hey, whoever lives there has been drinking kegs of beer while we've been drinking piss!"

"Let's find 'um and string 'um up!"

As they march toward the stairs, the chef crouches nervously. The footsteps up the stairs gradually become a distant echo. The chef gets up, leaves his bottles under the stairs and heads toward the barrel closest to the stairs. He licks the top of the barrel and exclaims "Ahlaalaa!!" He then rushes up the stairs in hopes of joining the angry posse.

Rhonna runs into them in the cell house hallway.

"Hey, where ya goin'?"

"On a beer run!"

Rhonna, in an 'Oh, what the hell' mood, caused by holiday imprisonment and worry, decides to join them in their quest.

"Yeah! I need a drink!" In the same breath, a soft whisper follows, *"I need to forget!"*

Rhonna follows the posse as they run down the zigzag path, stopping in back of the old barracks building.

"Where's the entrance?"

"Around the other side."

"Let's go!"

As they rush around to the other side, Rhonna leads the

way into the building.

"Where's the lights?"

"Here, let me through. I fixed the wiring in this building," Harold interrupts.

They rumble up the stairs, unbeknownst to the inhabitant on the third floor.

Inside room 314, the TV is blaring with crowd noise from the Rose Bowl.

"4th down and 2. Michigan is gonna go for it."

A woman presses the volume button on the remote with her left hand, while her right hand is curling a frosted mug of beer toward her mouth. Her left hand puts down the remote and picks up a cigar in the same motion. She lifts her head from the recliner.

"C'mon, stop that SOB!" she shouts at the screen.

As soon as Michigan crosses the goal line, she hears the sound of her door bursting open.

Harold, Rhonna, the red-haired man, and the man in overalls run into the smoky room.

"The counselor!!!" a few voices say in amazement.

She releases the cigar from her mouth. "What the hell are you doing here? There's no therapy session tonight!"

"Oh, yes there is," Harold insists as he waves his cohorts forward.

Pale and shaken, Goldie is outside the cell house, scanning the perimeter of the island for Rhonna. His mind has not fully processed the last half-hour's chain of events. The screaming, pushing and shoving, and fist fighting in the dining hall. The melee in the condo hallways. He had to hurdle over islanders who were wrestling, slapping and biting each other just to reach Rhonna's unit, but to no avail. Her vacant unit was ransacked. When he dashed outside the cell house, he called out to her. What echoed back was not her voice, but the disturbing crash of broken glass as some islanders were heaving rocks at the cell house's windows.

Is she injured in the riot? His thoughts are racing. As he pans the parade ground, he sees a naked man being chased by two women. Figures are dashing in and out of the old warden's house, yelling and smashing bottles. More figures rush out of the cell house. In an instant, Goldie is hit from behind and falls to the ground. As he slowly gets up, he sees a blur of islanders darting back and forth. He yells, "Rhonna!" But all that echoes back is a desperate call for help coming from the area around the sally port.

Goldie races down the zigzag path. As he jogs through the sally port, he sees figures huddled together in the distance. Could one of them be Rhonna? After jogging another hundred feet, it appears that some islanders are working on a construction project. Jogging closer, he now can discern the figures and what they are doing. His legs slow to a halt. He can hardly believe it. Rhonna is helping tie the therapist to wooden studs elevated over wooden barrels. His heart sinks.

"Rhonna, what the hell are you doing? Get away from her. All of you—what in the hell? Cut the crap!"

Harold looks at him and says, "Get the hell out of here, pretty boy!"

"Rhonna!" Goldie persists.

She looks toward Goldie and remains there frozen, listening.

"What do you think you're doing? This isn't fun. This isn't fun, dammit! She's gonna get hurt and you're part of it! What are you thinking of? Ah shit! Look at this place, look at you. This is all wrong." He turns around and starts to walk away.

Rhonna blurts out, "OK!" as she sticks a Cohiba in the counselor's mouth, and then walks toward him. His back is turned to her while he's walking. She starts to trot toward him crying out "Goldie, wait!" but he continues to walk. She runs in front of him. The look on her face is sad, her arms down, limbs weak. She has a look as if she has hit bottom.

"Goldie, please, I was just . . ."

"I can't believe you could take part in this kind of behavior. You said you don't belong here!"

"All right, I admit it. I crossed the line. But that counselor . . ."

"Well, she helped me!"

Goldie looks at Rhonna.

"No, she didn't. You . . ." She stops and slaps her hands to her side in frustration. Goldie continues to look at Rhonna as she stands in front of him.

"You're right, Rhonna." His voice begins to quiet as his head bows down. He looks up once again. "You did. I just didn't want you to be part of that." He takes her hands.

"Okay, Goldie, you just want me to be perfect."

"No. No . . . don't ever be, as long as we're together, don't ever be. You'll bore me to tears, and the rest of our life together will just be way too predictable," he chuckles.

Rhonna becomes silent.

"Oh, I didn't mean to imply that . . ."

Rhonna suddenly moves toward him and embraces him firmly, almost surprising him. She holds him there as her eyes begin to water.

"Goldie." She suddenly releases him from the embrace and tightly holds Goldie at arms length. "Goldie . . ." her voice weakens.

Meanwhile, Richie calls the patrol boat captain with his cell phone, and hurries toward the dock to meet him. He jumps on board a fifty-foot motor yacht; there are beautiful blondes waiting, all with drinks in their hands. The women have Santa hats on and all are singing Christmas carols. The half-lit captain is in a hurry to leave, but Richie explains they must stay and wait for one more islander. "Fire a flare!" Richie exclaims.

Back in the cell house, the door to Richie's unit is open. This time, because of the riot, she does not need to tiptoe into his room. Her eyes fixate on the sofa. As she hurries toward it, she does not see her object of desire. Her hands search the crevices of the sofa without luck. She looks around the sofa and on the end table standing next to it. Her desperate eyes dart around the room, landing on a small object lying on a bookshelf nearby. As she moves closer, the object takes the form of a pair of dark glasses. Her heart races as she quickly snatches them and heads back to the sofa.

She recaptures a previous pose on the sofa as her body is horizontal, with head tilted up a bit on the cushion. Tricia slowly slides on the glasses. A few deep breaths later, she now feels relaxed. Her arms sway a bit, waiting for something to happen. Nothing but darkness. She moves her head from side to side, then up and down, but still nothing. Her puzzled look is wiped away as she remembers how to start her VR experience. Her fingers attempt to press buttons on the frames, but the puzzled look returns. No buttons? In disbelief, her fingers impatiently strut up and down the frames. But the frames feel smooth. She quickly pulls off the glasses and examines them. She notices a label, "Revo," on the inside frame. "What? Sunglasses?" she yells as she flings them against the bookshelf. Her eyes resume scanning the room in hopes of finding the VR glasses.

"What the fuck are you doin' in my condo?" a voice booms.

Startled, Tricia turns around and sees the 18-year-old, decked out in a bathrobe, cigar in mouth, and holding what appears to be a bottle of wine. Her eyes zoom onto the label, a 1967 Chateau d'Yquem.

"What are YOU doin' here?" she sarcastically comments.

"Get the fuck out of here!" he replies with the cigar bobbing up and down in his mouth.

"That wine is worth more than you. Where the hell did you get it?"

"None of your damn business. Now get out or I'll wring your neck!"

Tricia scans the room. Her eyes catch another door leading into a small, enclosed space. Her feet follow her eyes as she heads toward what appears to be a closet. She opens the door, and searches for a light in this dark space. Her hand finds the light switch, and she finds another treasure. Racks upon rack of wine, a mini-wine cellar. Her mouth starts to salivate. Where should she start? In rapid-fire she pulls out several bottles: 1989, 1978, 1983, 2004, 1992, 1979, 1983, 1999. No luck. After each date is checked, the bottle is quickly loaded back in its slot. She randomly selects another row: 1990, 1976, 1954. Her eyes double-check the bottle with the prized vintage in her hand: 1954. She repeats out loud "Nineteen-fifty . . ." and a voice from behind continues, "Fore."

She turns around in time to see the 18-year-old winding up a golf club. She screams and quickly ducks as the golf club narrowly misses the top of her head. It continues its trajectory, colliding with a row of wine bottles in the rack behind her. Losing her balance, she falls to the floor, dropping the prized vintage, which adds a grand finale to the chorus of shattering glass.

"Damn," the 18-year-old sighs overlooking his once proud but now damaged wine-rack construction.

Tricia is already out the door and outside the unit, hobbling down the hallway.

"Damn, damn, damn," she echoes.

She sees a number of people flying down the hallway in both directions, and has to move out of the way to avoid being trampled by a gang of people. One of them is carrying a pair of binoculars that looks only too familiar to her. "Wait!" she screams and tries to hobble after them, but to no avail, as the gang is long past her. She turns back and hurries to her room. But on the way, a blood-colored splatter on another condo door stops her in her tracks. She slowly opens the door, and discovers more blood-colored stains that look like shotgun blasts on the walls, floor, and even ceiling. But where is the source of this? She grimaces at the thought of what she may find, but her curiosity drives her to open the bathroom door. Slowly, she turns the knob, and looks at the bathroom mirror to find the blood-colored pattern repeated there. Her eyes look down and spot several broken bottles, with labels such as "Cajun Squirts" and "Hot Rocks". Disappointed at her discovery, she slams the door and quickly exits the chef's unoccupied unit.

Approaching her unit, her mouth drops as she sees the door wide open. Rushing into her room, she focuses on the location of her buried treasure. Her eyes zoom onto her mattress, which is displaced from the box spring. "Oh my God!" she blurts out as she runs toward her bed. She moves the rest of the mattress off the box spring, but her prized possession, which she always hid under her mattress, is now gone. "My binoculars! Those animals!" she screams. She looks under her bed, but to no avail. Her eyes scan the entire room.

Directly in front of her, the dresser drawers are open and her clothes and underwear are strewn all over the dresser and floor. As she looks to the right, she screams as her eyes collide with her life-sized cardboard cutout of Leonardo DiCaprio. A pair of her panties is masked across his eyes like Zorro. Out of his mouth protrudes a rotten banana, while a pair of panty hose dangles from his legs. Her posters of Leonardo, hanging on the wall, are sliced as if by a Japanese steakhouse chef. An autographed framed photo of Leonardo on her nightstand has obscenities scrawled across it. But where is her model replica of the Titanic, which Leonardo personally signed and which was on her table? Feeling ill, she rushes to the bathroom and lifts the lid of the toilet seat. To her shock, she sees the Titanic model broken in two, sunken at the bottom of the toilet. Involuntarily, she vomits, covering up the Titanic in the now murky waters.

Back outside, one of the gang climbs up the guard tower and once at the top, glances through the binoculars and follows the flare's trail to the boat below. He yells, "There, over there, let's get the catapult," as he scales down the tower.

They hurry to the Agave Trail and move the rickety catapult into firing position, removing the shrubbery that surrounds it. The launching pad has recently been reinforced with many pieces of underwear, most noticeably bras, strung together. They load the catapult with a watermelon from a pile of ammunition on the bottom platform. Voice, who assists in setting up the catapult, stares at the women on the yacht through the binoculars and exclaims, "Look at the size of those melons."

The other man responds, "Yeah, they're the biggest I could find." They fire on the yacht, just missing.

Richie yells, "What was that?"

One of the women on his yacht says, "I didn't know there was fireworks, too."

Islanders load the catapult with cans of paint, and fire again. The yacht is hit, and paint is splattered everywhere. The women have green and red paint on various parts of their anatomy, and run into the cabin screaming. The captain and Richie are sliding on the paint and have a hard time keeping their balance. One islander is screaming, "A hit—a direct hit!"

But Voice complains, "We didn't sink it. Let's reload quick. This time with the good stuff!"

Hollering and rushing forward, the rioters push a creaky platform piled high with civil war era cannonballs toward the catapult. "Bring it on! Hurry!"

The captain is yelling, "They're after us! Let's move out!" But he is slipping and sliding, still struggling to remain on his feet. The islanders load the first cannonball onto the catapult, and adjust the arm to its lowest level. The first old ball is then fired, but misses its target, falling about five feet short. The splash is tremendous, and the captain and Richie are now soaking wet. Another is fired and lands even closer, just short of the stern. More ammunition is rapidly fired and with each splash, lands closer to its target.

As both Richie and the captain manage to finally get their balance, Richie says to the captain, "I'll steer; you hit the gas." With a burst of speed, they are out of firing range. Richie yells, "Stop it here, we're out of range."

But the captain retorts "Are you crazy, Richie? Let's go."

But Richie takes over the controls to stop the yacht just out of firing range, and yells to the captain, "Shoot up another flare!"

The Voice climbs in the catapult and yells, "Did you see him with those babes? They're gonna be mine! I'm gonna get him, I'm gonna get him, it's my only chance. I'll strangle him! Someone shoot me, shoot me!"

The gang laughs, and one adds "Does somebody wanna drag this pirate off?"

A different islander responds in a scraggily voice, "Argh, leave him on, Matey!" As they leave him screaming on the catapult, the Voice yells, "That's my ride, those are my women, let me at 'em!"

As the gang is ready to turn back, one of them hesitates. He does a double take, and exclaims "Oh, hell!" as he steps back to give the catapult lever a swift kick. The rest of the gang is frozen in wonder as they hear a loud noise, as if a giant mousetrap has been sprung, and then hear the scream "MAAA MAAAAAAAAAA!!!" whizzing through the air. A heavy Tinkerbelle has been launched, but the trajectory is not high enough to hit its mark. The Voice falls short of the target, making a splash about 20 feet from shore.

"Where the hell did he land?" one of the gang nervously inquires.

"Is he alive?"

"I saw a splash over there."

A few moments later, the Voice is heard emanating from the waters "it's !%!&#@&%%@#!&@!!$@@*!!!! freezing!"

But over the water there is another visual.

The flare. That is it. Richie's signal. Through all the commotion, Rhonna could still see it. It was bright red; the way she once imagined Santa's sleigh looked as it sailed across the sky. A bright red shooting star. Richie's flare meant there was no time to waste.

Goldie could see the red light reflected in her eyes. He quickly turns around and notices the upward trajectory of the flare. As he turns back toward her, a mixture of panic and excitement captures her.

"I have to go."

"Go where?"

She then mechanically turns around and heads toward the beach, without a reply.

"What the hell's goin' on?"

In a second, her silhouette shoots across the rocks down toward the dock. Rhonna breathes heavily, as she runs across the rugged landscape.

"Rhonna! Rhonna!" Goldie then cups his hand near his mouth to amplify his cry. "Rhonna!"

Rhonna didn't bother to turn her head. As he starts to lose sight of her in the darkness, he decides to chase her. He runs toward her and trips. As he gets up, he sees a small green light at the water's edge. Her silhouette jumps toward it.

That was it, she was on her way. He wondered where.

"Rhonna!" In an impulsive moment, he jumps into the water and tries to swim a few strokes, and with every stroke he pushes a lifetime behind him. The boat moves swiftly away, farther and farther out of reach. As he realizes it's a futile attempt, he becomes aware of the freezing waters. He flashes back to his trip to the island, but this time, no maiden to hang onto. He swims back to the dock, swallowing some of the choppy waters on the way. As he pulls himself onto the dock, he is exhausted, freezing, and looks at the ocean, with only a dim green light visible in the distance. He does not hear the sound of a helicopter descending.

Rhonna needed to, but couldn't look back. She is now sitting in the cabin of the yacht, wrapped in a blanket courtesy of Richie. The island is outside of her view. Her head hangs low, thinking of what might have been. But she reminds herself of the dire need of her mother, and of a new world revolving around family. Will she be able to handle this level of responsibility? She glances down and notices that she has been turning the rings on her fingers. She flashes back to the first time she met Goldie after the therapy session, when she was doing the same. His sensitivity, his vulnerability, his . . .

She turns the rings around her fingers a bit more and remembers their walks together, and how his golden tooth sparkled in the sun. How special were their intimate moments in the solitary cell. What did she leave behind? Her hands now cover her eyes, and tears are escaping through the spaces between her fingers.

Inside the hovering helicopter, Santa Claus is holding a bottle of Coca-Cola in portrait style. His cheeks are red, and he is belting out Christmas carols. The pilot is begging for him to stop singing, "Charlie, it's 'omnipotent' not 'impotent.'"

But Santa continues his refrain. He bends over, grabs a bottle of rum, and pours it into his Coke while slurring, "Forever and ever, Hallelujah! Hallelujah! . . ." The 'copter light has just reached the island.

"We're about there, Charlie."

Santa hesitates for a moment and looks in his bag. "And what does Santa have for all you little A-holes down there?" He brushes his hand against his beard, which is now pulled to one side. He suddenly thrusts the door open.

"Hey, what the hell are you doing?" the pilot yells.

"HOle! HOle! HOle! Merry Christmas!" Santa bellows, oblivious to the pilot.

"Close that . . ."

But before the pilot could finish his sentence, the bag is heaved out of the side door. It bounces off some rocks on the island near the bay side, and the letters spill out like confetti onto the waters below. The pilot circles back, aiming the 'copter's light into the bay.

"Gosh darn. Next year we're gonna subcontract a Santa."

But as the light is searching for the mail, it slices across an object floating in the bay. The helicopter moves in closer to the object, which takes on a human form.

"Oh my God, it can't be! It's a person!"

Santa now replies, "I didn't know there were any people there. I thought there was just A-holes."

The pilot quickly grabs his radio. "Red tag . . . red tag . . . 14 point 75 latitude. Person floating in bay about 100 feet from Alcatraz. May Day." He turns toward Santa, who is now passed out. "We gotta notify the mayor!"

The mayor is at a Christmas Eve party, which is attended by many politicians. He is in a secluded room with his campaign manager. As he backs her onto his leather couch, she whispers, "Do you think now is the best time? Your wife is downstairs talking to the governor."

"Oh, oh, it's OK, it's OK," as he buries his mouth in her neck.

Moments later, she squeezes a cylindrical shaped object in his pants; unaware it is one of his finest Cuban cigars.

"We'll smoke afterwards," he says.

Suddenly she jerks back. "It's beeping!"

"Whhhaaattt?"

"It sounds like it's coming from your crotch."

"My WHAT?" he mumbles. He starts to open his eyes and realizes what she is saying. "Oh, damn!" He slowly releases his embrace and checks his cell phone. He presses a button to auto-callback.

A panicked voice on the other end asks, "Mayor?"

"Damn, what is this?"

"It hit the fan on Traz!"

"What the hell? What are you talking about?"

"The counselor's floating in the bay."

"What?"

"We've got a boat picking her up, but it looks like a riot, sir."

There is a period of silence as he springs off the sofa, inadvertently causing his campaign manager to fall to the floor, taking the mayor with her.

Downstairs, the governor glances up. "Did you hear something fall?" The mayor's wife stares at the ceiling.

The mayor speaks into his watch. "I'll meet you in my office in five minutes." He turns to his manager. "I'll be back in ten minutes, honey."

When he enters the office, his advisor says in a stern voice, "I was expecting something to happen. I'm surprised it took this long." He proceeds to explain the little he knows of the situation.

"Who knows about this?"

"At this moment, the helicopter pilot, the Coast Guard, and Santa."

"Who?"

"But I wouldn't worry too much about Santa; he's too damned hammered to . . . Look, in about an hour a handful of reporters will know. By morning the whole city will be aware of this."

"It'll look like I've lost control!" The mayor's eyes shift wildly while he nervously chews on his lower lip. "Listen, get the Coast Guard NOW! It's your job to make sure nothing leaks. Rotate the cameras on these assholes, I've gotta see this for myself."

A few moments later, the fifty-foot screen on the Alcatraz dock is filled with the image of the mayor. No islanders are paying any attention. Simultaneously from the mayor's conference screen, figures are seen darting back and forth across the island. The mayor says, "I knew we should have put more cameras on the island."

The advisor responds, "Your orders were to only equip the perimeter of the island, with cameras pointing outward."

"Ahh, shit. Gimme the microphone." A voice is projected from the screen on the island. "Now hear this . . . this is the mayor. If this rioting does not stop, I will be forced to send armed guards to restore peace."

Harold grabs a baseball bat and runs about 20 feet in front of the screen. The mayor sees a balding, bulging, middle-age man yelling, "Cover your balls, fagboy!!!" With the slow toss of a ball and a swing of the bat, the mayor and his advisor see a white flash approaching with the speed of a comet, a glimpse of a red seam, and the ball disappears to the left of the screen. Harold picks up another ball, takes a large swing, and misses the ball. "I'm hitting like your mom, Mayor." The next ball is tossed up and with a ferocious swing; the ball barely dribbles a few feet in front of the screen. "Ahh, screw it." He walks toward the screen, and in a moment the bat is hurled through the air. In a reflex movement, both the mayor and his advisor step backward and cover their faces as the image of the bat enlarges as it reaches the screen. The last words are heard from the monitor, "Up your . . .", as suddenly the screen goes black with the sound of a loud crash.

"Son-of-a-bitch!" the mayor exclaims. "What the shit is this?" he gasps as he looks at another screen, where Big Boy is making noises. He cups his hand under his arm and flaps with his other arm, continuing to make obscene noises. Then he takes off his shirt and wiggles his large breasts, which are bouncing closer to the screen.

"Turn off screen 5, dammit!"

On another screen a catapult is seen in the distance, being loaded with an old porcelain prison toilet. A scruffy man near the catapult screams, "Fire!" as the heavy projectile sails gracefully into the bay, a hundred feet from the camera. "Adjust 20 degrees!" shouts the scruffy man, as the catapult is turned in line with the camera. As soon as the catapult is reloaded, this time with several bottles of Cajun sauce, the voice yells, "Fire!" Bottles are in the air flying everywhere, with one bottle hitting its target, the camera.

As the Mayor and advisor see the screen go blank, the mayor shouts, "Damn animals! They'll pay for this!"

"Mayor, I'll call the guard. Peace needs to be restored as soon as . . ."

"Remember, I don't care who the hell gets hurt or killed. It cost us millions restoring this island. Make sure no harm comes to these buildings!"

"But, Mayor . . ."

"Listen, have the guards surround the buildings at strategic points. You know the island. If anyone damages property, bust their heads!"

"But sir . . ."

"Does anyone else know about this?"

"No, sir."

"Good, let's keep it that way. I have to make a personal visit. I'll be right back."

Following his orders, troops are dispatched immediately and begin congregating at Pier 33. A photographer, recording scenes of Alcatraz from the Golden Gate Bridge, notices the commotion. He picks up a cell phone.

"Nick?"

"Yep, what's up, Enrique?"

"Where are you?"

"At Fisherman's Wharf. What's up?"

"Good, you're only a minute away. Come quickly. There's some group of uniformed men huddled together at Pier 33. Looks like they may be boarding the Harbor Empress soon."

"Be there in a New York minute."

The photographer turns his lens toward the group of men. In a minute, they begin boarding the Empress. As the last uniformed man boards, the reporter in street clothes, coming out of nowhere, runs toward the Empress and jumps on the outside railing of the boat—just in time. The photographer's lens follows the action while the boat heads for Alcatraz.

His focus is steady as he whispers in a Spanish accent, "Have a nice ride, my friend."

As the boat disappears in the darkness, the photographer packs up his equipment and shakes his head. He looks toward Alcatraz, and says, "Trazzzz. My friend, I would not want your job."

As the boat lands at the island's pier, the guards rush onto the island and the stranger waits for all to go ashore before jumping over the rail. Under his jacket are a microphone and other electronic equipment. Prisoners are still running wild, and screams are reverberating throughout the island. The guards take their positions around the cell house, inside the hallways of the prison, in the dining hall, and around the perimeters of the doctor's and counselor's dwellings.

The reporter first sees a man in a chef's hat and white gown doubled up, nose bleeding, screaming "Ah eee Ah eee!" A frying pan is beside him. In the corner of the dock, a stone-faced guard watches them as he lights up a cigarette. People are still darting back and forth across the island.

"Oh, my God!" the reporter shouts in amazement as he notices some commotion in the bay. He zooms in as Coast Guard rescuers are untying the counselor from the raft. He pulls a phone from his pocket, and yells, "Hey, Jim, I'm sending you the pictures now." He reaches in his bag of equipment and pulls out a portable camera, and then pans the island.

Back at the Channel 6 control room, a mad scramble ensues as everyone jockeys for position near the large screen. The chief editor and the crew witness the scene. "Good feed!" Jim yells on his speakerphone. "We're goin' live—3 . . . 2 . . . 1 . . . NOW!"

Across all monitors in the country, the news interrupts the normal programming in progress. On the monitors, the word "TRAZ" appears in bold black letters against a blood-red background. The character of the graphics suggests bloodshed, and an alarming voice calls out, "Riot on Alcatraz. No word on casualties. Here's dramatic footage of guards rescuing an innocent victim of the brutal massacre taking place—she's barely breathing, being rescued from drowning in the bay."

The viewing public catches what's really happening. With a close camera angle, the counselor's face looks wretched as she shrieks, "What took you so long? My ass is face down in the bay and you two brownies can't undo a square knot!" She tosses her wet cigar at one of them and says "Ahh, crap, somebody get me a dry cigar."

When the mayor returns to the Christmas party, he sneaks back to the secluded room.

"Grace, something came up. I can't stay."

She then sighs, "Oh, hon, it's nothin' we can't take care of later."

"But . . . but . . ."

"No buts now."

She pulls him down and her buttocks hits the monitor's remote control. Suddenly the TV blares, "Riot in Alcatraz."

The mayor pops up and screams, "God bless it!" He rushes out of the room and jumps into his limo. "My office. Move!" he yells to the driver. He pulls his cell phone out and calls his office. "Get Jack, Henry and Kelly. In my office in a minute."

Meanwhile, the mayor's campaign manager runs a few steps and sticks her head out the door as she yells, "What's goin' on?" But he is long gone. As she heads back into her apartment, she is about to turn off the TV when suddenly the screen turns completely black. Displayed on the screen a second later is dripping blood with skull images. "Traz—countdown to carnage." She immediately passes out.

The mayor is now in his office, and turns toward his advisor as he hollers, "What are we gonna do? How did the story break?"

The advisor shakes his head and calmly states, "At this

point, we don't know. The roving reporter broke the story from Traz. How he got on, we don't know. At this moment the guards on the island are trying to locate him."

The mayor yells, "Maybe he flew in with the Birdman of Alcatraz. Turn those damn cameras around. I don't want anyone else getting on. Find his ass and get it off the island. Is there any jamming device to prevent communications from the island?"

"No."

"Here we go," he says as the phone rings. "Unplug the damn thing."

"Yes sir, Mayor, but you'll need to comment quickly on the situation and pretend it's under control."

The mayor says angrily, "You handle the media and set up the press conference. Where's Kelly?"

"Umm," a voice murmurs.

"Where the hell is he? I need my press manager."

"Mayor, sir, he's at a Christmas party, and uh, he sounded pretty inebriated when we called."

"Damn! Call what's-his-name."

At that instant, one of his aides looks up at screen 6, and says surprisingly "Jet ski."

"No, it wasn't a Polack name like Jetski. I think it was a Dago name."

The aide says hurriedly, "No, I mean up there," as he points to screen 6. Everyone turns around as they see a man dressed as Santa Claus on a jet ski, heading straight toward Alcatraz.

The mayor interjects, "Son of a bitch!" Everyone now pans the six screens, three of which are still operational. On screen 1 another boat is seen heading toward the island, with a man on water skis in back of the boat. The few unbroken cameras show various boats, both large and small, heading toward the island.

The mayor grabs the framed portrait of his wife and heaves it toward screen 6. It misses its target, but hits screen 5 instead, as the screen explodes.

"Mayor, should I pick up the pieces?"

But the mayor ignores him, and quickly grabs his cell phone.

"This is the mayor. Do not let anyone on the island. I repeat, do not let anyone on the island. Abandon your current positions and guard the perimeter of the island with your lives. Do you read me?" After a few seconds, the mayor asks, "How many boats are there?" After a hesitation, "What? Freakin' morons! Use your bullhorns to threaten them. Tell them you'll use firepower." He then abruptly hangs up.

"What are we gonna do? There are dozens of boats near Traz."

"We can try calling more guards, but Mayor, it's Christmas Eve and I don't think we can get many more."

"Threaten them. Fire the guards that don't show up. How 'bout the Marines?"

"Mayor, sir, we're not exactly taking Iwo Jima."

"I pay you assholes lots of money, now give me some advice."

"Sir, we're calling the reserve guards and troopers. We have some boats circling the island to cut off invaders. Right now we can just keep up."

"How about the National Guard?"

"Yes, Mayor."

Back on the island, the prisoners run rampant in the old cell house. The door to Richie's condo is open, and the sound of a crowd cheering bursts forth from the unit. The Cubs fan is hurrying through the hallway on the way to his room, intent on barricading himself inside.

He hesitates as he passes Richie's doorway, but continues his brisk pace. Suddenly, from the opening of the doorway he hears, "Collect this memento from the Chicago Cubs' historic season." He back-peddles quickly and steps inside the room to discover a flat panel display covering the entire wall, with an infomercial showing the faces of all the Cubs players on a pennant. "You, too, can have this autographed pennant with all your favorite Cubbies on it. Quantities are limited, so act now! Also included is this video of the Cubs play-off drive." The screen now displays a Cubs player hitting a home run. The fan's face now turns pale. "Relive them winning the World Series, culminating with Trey Griffey's clutch grand slam in the bottom of the ninth of game seven!" Upon hearing this, the fan screams, "They did it! My God, they did it!" A moment later he screams, "I missed it! My God, I missed it!" With this he clutches his chest, stumbles out of the room, and falls to the ground.

On the dock, the reporter's camera pans the scene. The reporter's tongue passes from one side of his mouth to the other, as if in expectation of filet mignon. "Broadway, Times Square, Solitary, here I come!" he exclaims as he zigzags up the island to the old cell house entrance. He knows exactly where to go, as he rehearsed this path many times in his mind. Near the old cell house, he looks up and says in awe, "Just like I pictured it!" Out of breath, he runs in the entrance, and heads toward "A" block. No one is in the hallway, so he scampers to "B" block—Broadway. At the end of the aisle, there's some commotion. He darts to the end of the hallway and squirms between a few people, as he demands, "Move back, move back!" Now at the front, he sees a man with a Cubs hat and sweatshirt sprawled on the floor, motionless. "What happened?" the reporter anxiously asks.

A female voice in the crowd softly says, "He's dead."

Another voice in the crowd yells out in a mock Harry Carey voice, "HOLY COW!"

The Circus

Local news has given way to national news, as TV screens across the country flash, "1 person killed, many injured in riot on Alcatraz."

The image of the man in Cub fatigues, sprawled helplessly, is also shown on multiple screens in all of the casinos in Las Vegas. In the Flamingo Hilton, a hush descends over the sports bar. Then on the electric tote board, a flashing starburst on the screens displays the words, "1 DEAD" in neon orange. A ticker below displays the following message: "Flash! Deathline . . . 1–4 victims on Traz 2:1 . . . 5–10 victims on Traz 3:1 . . . More than 10 killed 4:1 . . . PLAY DEATHLINE AND WIN! WIN! WIN!"

The silence breaks and the bettors immediately clamor to the betting windows. At the window, one of the bettors asks the teller, "There's no coverage on Traz. How do we know if we won?"

The teller responds in a gravelly voice, "They found out one guy cashed in, didn't they?"

"Does that include guards, too?"

"Yep."

"OK, then $200 on, let's see, 5–10 victims."

"Good luck," the man says as he hands him the ticket and smiles.

"I think I'll give this ticket to my grandma—she did time in the Houston pen."

Back in the mayor's office, the dead Cubs fan is flashed on the screens.

"Son of a bitch! I ordered the fuckin' reporter off the island!" the mayor bellows.

"They are still searching for him, sir," his advisor answers apologetically.

"All those guards, and they can't find one pansy-ass reporter. Maybe I should've sent the Marines." He shakes his head in disgust and pounds his fist on his desk. "I want two hundred officers shipped to Alcatraz immediately."

"But sir, you'll deplete our forces here in San Francisco. You'll be inviting crime . . ."

"Shut up and do as I say!"

"Yes, sir."

Pounding on the mayor's door becomes louder, with a hungry mob yelling and begging to get in. Only a newspaper editor and a TV newscaster are escorted in by the mayor's entourage.

"Mayor, as you know, we're the number one paper in this city. But our circulation has been a little low. We could use this scoop," the bespeckled editor pleads.

The mayor retorts, "You're wasting my time. You know the law."

The newspaper editor replies in a voice as soft as butter, "Your last election was close, Mayor. Our company not only owns the *Chronicle,* but also Channel 17."

The mayor shoots back, "Where the hell were you guys last election? You backed that lesbo Mrs. Dyke, and now you need my help?"

"Mayor, the polls show the next race much closer."

The mayor's brow softens as he rubs his chin. His advisor interrupts the silence by clearing his throat and takes the mayor to the side. His voice accelerates as he warns the mayor, "Look, endorsements won't mean a damn thing if you lose control now."

The mayor's brow once again rises as he booms, "Please escort these gentlemen out."

As they are tossed from the room, the editor screams, "You'll be sorry!"

"What am I gonna say to that damn mob?" The mayor looks to his cohorts. They all huddle together around the mayor's desk to brief him.

As his aides clear a path to a podium in the conference room, the mayor is bombarded by a slew of questions. As he sits down and straightens his tie, he calmly summarizes the situation.

"There has been a death on Alcatraz tonight, the cause of which will be thoroughly investigated. Due to recent unrest on this island, the Coast Guard has been called in and has restored peace and safety on Alcatraz. No other casualties have been reported. Everything is under control."

A reporter stands up and fires a question a few decibels above the crowd's inquiries. "Mayor, the live feed from Alcatraz seems to indicate a full-blown riot, with some people bloodied. Are there any injuries?"

"Not to our knowledge. Nothing beyond a few minor cuts or bruises."

More hands and voices rise from the back, but an aide breaks in. "This concludes the press conference."

As the mayor walks away from the podium, he nudges his advisor and whispers to him from the side of his mouth "All this bullshit because of some loser." As he glides back into his office followed by his aides, he yells to them, "Turn on the tubes. All your heads will roll if I see any more shit on these tubes."

In San Francisco, a little girl excitedly jumps out of bed. Her heart is pounding in expectation of Santa's treasures under her tree. Will she see the hover bike she has been asking for all year? And how about DNA-Dollie? And Bio-Bobby?

She pulls the covers to the side and runs into the living room. To her dismay, there is nothing under the tree. Her heart sinks. She darts to her Christmas stocking, which is hanging from the fireplace mantle. As she presses the stocking, she feels nothing inside. Sadly she turns around and scans the living room. The TV is blaring, there are a few cans of beer on the end table that reflect the multi-colored lights from the Christmas tree, and her dad is snoring on the sofa. As she runs over to her dad, she yanks at his sleeve. No movement. She pulls again and yells, "Daddy, Daddy, did Santa come?" But her father only turns on his side with his back to her, still sound asleep. "Daddy, Daddy!" she cries, but to no avail. She finally grabs the remote and turns the volume all the way up. She covers her ears with her tiny hands, and her father finally awakens from his deep sleep.

"What the hell?" he mumbles as he turns to his side.

"Daddy, Daddy, did Santa come?"

Unable to hear her, he looks for the remote, finally seeing it in his daughter's hand. He grabs it away from her and turns the volume down as he shouts, "What do you think you're doing?"

"Daddy, Daddy, did Santa come?"

"No, not yet. Now go to bed!" he barks at her. As he is about to turn off the TV, his eyes catch the scene of Santa parachuting toward Alcatraz. His eyes are now glued to the TV, and, as his daughter sees this, she also turns toward the TV.

On the screen a woman excitedly pants, "We are waiting for the latest word from Alcatraz. How many more A-holes will be casualties?"

The father's jaw drops. His daughter looks up at her dad and asks innocently, "Daddy, is that where mommy stays?"

Above the island, the skies become busy with story-breaking opportunists. Two low flying helicopters are competing with each other for a story. They are flying dangerously close to each other. A man on one ladder knocks a camera out of the hands of a reporter dangling from the other copter's ladder. Higher in the sky, somebody parachutes out of a plane and plunges into the water. A man in a jet pack almost descends on the island, but has to keep circling because he cannot find a good place to land. Missing the cellhouse roof, he ends up crashing into the Water Tower.

Back at the mayor's office, one monitor now shows the 18-year-old being interviewed on Alcatraz. Other monitors follow the circus of the helicopters, boats, and parachutists trying to land on the island.

The mayor is beyond enraged as he yells "Another fuckin' reporter?"

An aide calmly states, "Sir, it's been hard for our guards and police to sort out the prisoners from the reporters."

Another aide excitedly adds "How about the red 'A'?"

The mayor returns a puzzled look.

"You know, Mayor, the red 'A'. Remember, it wasn't just for humiliation purposes."

"Oh, yeah. The red 'A.'" He quickly picks up his cell phone. "This is the mayor. I order you to check everyone's buttocks." After a second he yells, "No buts about it." After a few more seconds, the mayor continues, "Now listen here. Everyone without a red 'A' on their ass, get 'em off the island. Report to me when you have finished this assignment." He throws his phone on the desk.

On the island, the shakedown is beginning. A flashlight spots a few islanders running through the parade ground. Rifles are cocked.

"Hold it there!"

But the figures continue running, until finally warning shots are fired in the air. The figures suddenly freeze, and through a bullhorn a voice booms, "Pull down your pants for the inspection."

"What?"

As the figures stare into the rifle barrels, they slowly turn around and follow the order.

"Remove your underwear, also" the bullhorn spouts.

As their underwear is reluctantly removed amidst moaning and groaning, the flashlight reflects off the first set of derrieres. A red "A" shines. Now the flashlight moves to the next set, reflecting another "A." The light now moves to the last set, revealing a mark. One guard inquires to the other "Is that an 'A'?" As the flashlight moves closer to the quivering cheeks, the mark becomes a cluster of pimples. A few guards now approach this figure and frisk him.

"What the hell is goin' on?" the figure stutters. In his shirt they discover a palm-size recorder, which they confiscate.

"Take him away," the bullhorn shouts.

"Where are you taking me?" the man shouts, as he is handcuffed. "I have rights!" he continues, but is quickly escorted to the dock by a few armed guards.

After the island has been searched for an hour by a few hundred police and guards, the police chief relays a message to the mayor, who anxiously answers the phone.

"Mission complete, Mayor."

"Mission complete?"

"Yes, sir. We have five reporters detained."

"Where did you find them?"

"Two in the old cell house. One on the southeastern end of the island. Another in the recreation yard. And the last one, sir, I don't think he is too bright. He tried to interview one of our officers."

"Did you search all the buildings?"

"Yes, sir. Everything from the old industries building on the northwestern end to the barracks on the southeastern end."

"Comb the island one more time."

"No problem. What should we do with the detainees?"

"Do you know where the holding cells on Water Street are?"

"Affirmative."

"I want them transported there. Strip search them, confiscate all their equipment, and keep them there until I tell you otherwise. Is the island totally sealed off?"

"Yes, sir. We have a shield of police and guards around the perimeter. And we have more than enough security personnel monitoring the other parts of the island."

"I better not see any more interviews on TV."

"No, sir."

"Maintain your positions until I tell you otherwise."

"Yes, sir."

As he hangs up the phone, one of his aides picks up the remote and points it at the monitors, which are currently showing a few boats still attempting to reach the island.

"What the hell are you doin'?" the mayor interjects.

A street scene now flashes on the monitors. A young woman is chewing gum in the foreground and a street vendor is pulling lobsters from a bin in the background. A microphone is shoved in front of the young woman's face.

"Do you think the island is safe? What should be done with the prisoners?"

The young woman pulls the wad of gum from her mouth and tosses it nonchalantly on the sidewalk.

"I definitely think the island is unsafe because of the rioting. The prisoners shouldn't stay there. More people could get killed."

The camera zooms in on the man in the background, who is holding a lobster in each fist.

"Sir, do you think the island is safe? What should be done with the prisoners?"

The man clears his throat, and with a sincere voice says, "No, no, no. Too many people getting their heads busted." He turns his head, squints his eyes, and softly says, "Excuse me, Miss. What was the second question?"

"What should be done with the prisoners?"

"They should get them off the island." He then flashes a bright smile as he points to a sign behind him. "And then march them right on to Sammy's Seafood, the best seafood place in town. Fresh fish caught . . ."

The aide turns off the monitors, and turns to the mayor. "The polls, sir, are you aware of the polls?"

But the mayor isn't listening.

Another aide says to the mayor, "We've looked at the latest polls on the Internet from the major news agencies. Here's what they're saying: 78% of the people think the island is unsafe and want the islanders removed. 67% don't want any more of their taxpayer money going toward maintaining the island or keeping the prisoners on the island."

The mayor's face turns a deeper shade of red. "I thought I told everyone things are under control. There's no more reporters on the island and no more rioting."

"Sir, you know how the media spins things. The people are also concerned with the cost of keeping a lot of police and guards on the island."

"What do we do?" he asks, as he throws his hands up in the air.

The advisor states, "Unfortunately, 98% of the people polled don't want the islanders back in San Francisco."

"We're in a Catch-22 situation," the mayor whines. "What are our options?"

"Sir, we're still looking into our options."

"Get outta here and find me those options."

"Yes, sir."

As his staff hurries out of the office, the mayor rubs his eyes and shakes his head. His private phone rings, and the caller ID reveals his home number. Thinking it's his wife, he lets the phone continue ringing. Reaching into his pocket, he pulls out a bottle of Trazadone. His trembling hands attempt to open the bottle, but to no avail. He clenches his teeth around the lid and snaps it open, spitting the lid onto the floor. Emptying the jar into his mouth, he reaches for the water pitcher. Not a drop of water. As the bitter pills dissolve in his mouth, his eyes desperately search the office. Grabbing the fishbowl on his desk with two hands, he takes a few gulps of water to wash the medicine down.

"God, why me?" the mayor says as he lays his head down on his desk, overcome by exhaustion. He nods off to sleep. Twenty minutes pass by, and he is snoring with his head resting between his cradled arms. Suddenly, a door opens and a voice cuts through the silence.

"Mayor."

At this the mayor slowly lifts his head and rubs his eyes.

"What?"

"Did I wake you?"

The mayor's vision is still blurred, and he rubs his eyes again. But the dimly lit room reveals little about the dark figure.

"Who is it?" the mayor's voice trembles.

"I am the Ghost of Christmas Present," the voice deepens.

The mayor's brow sharpens and his eyes squint. All he can discern is the open hand of an outstretched arm. The fingers seem to glow, reflecting light as if a hundred diamonds surround it. At the end of the manicured fingertips hangs a pair of glasses. They also seem to glow, with a subtle blue light. Sweat is dripping from the mayor's brow, and chills are running through his body. He feels unsure if he is awake or if this is a continuation of a dream. Suddenly the figure steps forward from the shadows.

"Richie!" the mayor exclaims.

"I want you to look at something, some *place* I should say," Richie calmly answers.

"What?"

Richie firmly states, "Try them on."

The mayor looks puzzled at the glasses in Richie's hands.

His face changes expression as he now realizes what Richie is holding.

"What are these 'X-ray specs'? Can I bring these home? It's the only way I'll get to see my wife naked," he jokes. "Why, what is it—are these VR lenses? I've heard about all that stuff. Look, this doesn't impress me. I'm in the here and now, the real. This stuff is fun but I'm in the middle of a crisis. Maybe we can set something up after this situation is under control . . . I mean over."

"Take a look. This situation *is* over."

"What?" he asks curiously. "Give me those things."

The mayor starts to grab at them as Richie gladly hands them over with a smile, a deal-closing smile, all too familiar with his business partners. Richie looks at the expression on the mayor's face as he places them over his eyes. The mayor starts to smile.

"Hey, this is pretty nice . . . beautiful colonial mansions. It's like I'm really there. This place is gorgeous . . . do you mind if I walk around, I mean move around a bit?" As he speaks, a red light on the side of the frames flashes like lightning. "Tell me Richie, where is this? What does this have to do with me?" He starts to reach for the glasses as if to remove them when Richie firmly stops his hand with his own.

"John," Richie says in a quiet, almost hypnotic monotone, "this is Alcatraz." His smile reappears. There is no flashing red light dancing off of the glasses, just the blue glow remains, but as the mayor's eyebrows rise with surprise, he tries to reach for something. His head turns and he reaches again.

"Reality," whispers Richie as he punches some numbers

into the keypad. "Take your time. I've had a survey team take a very close look at this."

The mayor moves his head up, then down, then in a circle. As he pulls off the glasses, he naively remarks, "Richie, I'm not sure what you're getting at."

"John, I know you like things to the point."

Richie walks toward the door and flips a light switch, which causes floodlights to shine upon the wall opposite the mayor's desk. He struts toward the well-lit wall, which displays the map of the United States. Richie's finger now points toward a dot off the coast of California.

"This is what I want. Alcatraz will be *the* island resort," Richie boasts.

Richie's finger now softly glides to the right ever so slightly.

"John, here's what you get."

At this, the mayor leans forward in his chair.

"You get San Francisco again. If you thought my campaign contributions were generous in your last election, you ain't seen nothin' yet."

The mayor's jaw drops and his eyes widen.

"Richie, don't get me wrong. This sounds great, but there's one problem. What do we do with all those assholes?"

Richie's finger lifts off the map, and, as he walks a few steps to the right, it touches down again.

"New York City?" the mayor's voice cracks.

"Yes. They can finish their sentences in NYC. As I recall, the Mayor of New York City owes you and I a little favor. His brother wouldn't have the position or the property in San

Francisco if it wasn't for us."

"You think he'd do it?"

Richie motions toward the phone.

The mayor presses a few numbers on his speaker phone. When the call is answered, the mayor says enthusiastically, "Bill, got a favor to ask you."

"Hey, I heard on the news about the riot."

"Well, it's related to that. I'll cut to the chase. Can these A-holes finish out their term somewhere in New York City?"

"You've got to be kidding me. We've got more than our share of jerks here already."

The mayor turns toward Richie, then back again at the phone.

"Remember when you said if I ever need anything . . . after I got your brother in here as President of the Board? Hey, I'll even throw in one thousand of the finest Cuban cigars for you and your boys. They're $100 apiece on the black market."

An awkward moment of silence follows.

"What brand?"

"Cohibas"

"It's a little too mild for me. Can you get either Juervo Ciuo or Juentos Mio? They have a stronger flavor."

"No problem."

"OK. Make it two thousand—a thousand of each—and you have yourself a deal."

"You drive a hard bargain."

"Just so you know, they'll be living in the Hole in Harlem. We've got plenty of vacant, burned-out buildings there."

"I don't care where the hell they live, as long as it ain't here."

"With all the murders, rapes and sick crimes in Harlem, your A-holes will look like Girl Scouts."

"Hope you don't mind if Richie and I light up a Ciero Blanco to celebrate the deal."

"Richie, are you there too? Good! Hey, I got one Imperial left. I'll join you."

Before the mayor can reach into his pocket, Richie's 24-carat gold lighter is already lighting his cigar. As they puff away, the mayor blurts, "Excuse me for a second, Bill" and presses another button on his phone to reach his advisor.

"Henry, I want you and the boys to coordinate getting all the prisoners off of Alcatraz immediately. They are to be transported to Harlem. That's right, Harlem. You know the mayor's assistants there. Contact them immediately so you guys can work out the logistics. Get a press conference set up for me first thing in the morning . . . that's right."

His finger presses another button on the phone, which switches him back to the NYC mayor.

"Hey, is it true the sun never sets in New York City? What the hell is that about?"

"Yep. It's bright as daylight here all the time. Well, our guys studied it and found there'd be less crime in daylight. With the lost production time because of muggings and murders and whatnot, they decided the spots should always stay on. And the insurance companies are happy, too. But you should see our electric bill."

"Remind me not to vacation there."

"Yeah, I gotta get outta this shit hole. Did the Mayor of West Palm Beach die yet?"

"He's older than Florida. But seriously, if you ever want to get away I just found a good resort for you."

Back at Alcatraz the guards use bullhorns to send the message to the islanders.

"Urgent! Urgent! All A-holes who want to leave the island, board the boat by the dock in 10 minutes. I repeat, all A-holes who want to leave the island, board the boat by the dock in 10 minutes. All others will remain on this island indefinitely."

There is a mad scramble in the old cell house. Clothes are being shoved in suitcases in all the condos on the island. All but one . . .

A figure stands over a steep, rocky ledge overlooking the bay. He unknowingly escaped the flashlights just an hour earlier, for he appeared to blend in with the rocks. The water shimmers from the lighthouse beam, but is blurry through his teary-eyed view. He shrugs his shoulders, and breathes a heavy sigh.

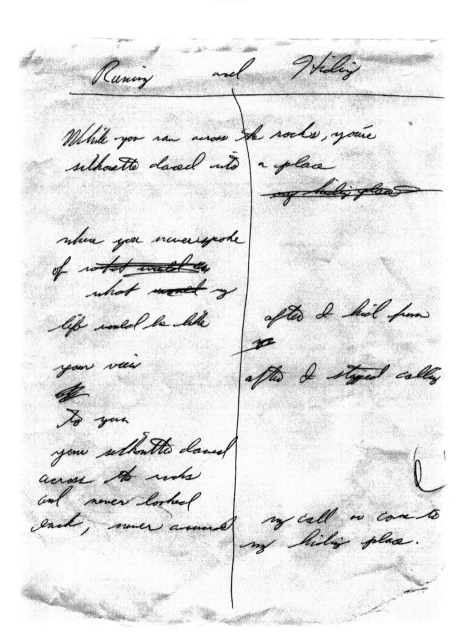

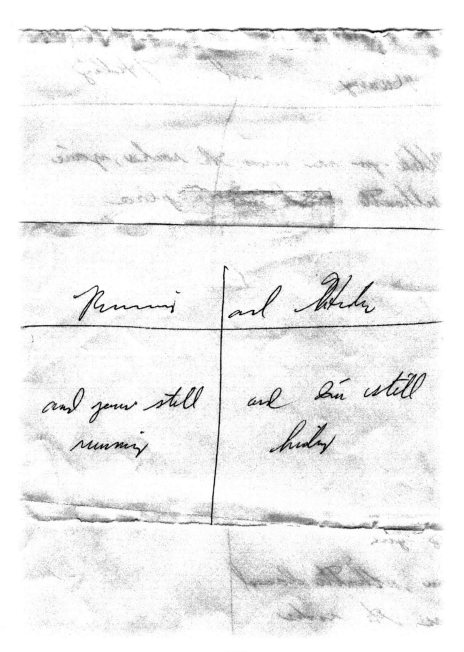

As he inches closer to the edge, some rocks loosen beneath his feet and begin a slow-motion descent into the dark waters below. Any closer and the figure will follow the same downward path, and be swallowed up in the bay. As he is about to take his last step forward, someone taps him on the shoulder. He is jolted back to the present, and turns around. It is the priest, who puts his arm around Goldie's shoulder. "Let's hurry, there's only five minutes left."

"I'm not going. You go ahead." But the priest does not budge.

"You'll miss the boat," Goldie asserts. Still the priest does not move.

"You won't leave without me, will you?" In response, the priest shakes his head from side to side. "Look, you don't understand my life . . ." Suddenly Goldie stops talking as he looks toward the dock and realizes the boat will leave within minutes. "Okay, Father, let's go." Goldie grabs the priest's hand, pulls him swiftly away from the ledge, and scurries toward the boat.

As they approach the dock, the boat's horn blows. Dozens of feet are scampering to get in the boat. A limping Cajun chef, a bloodied and crawling Tricia, a soaking wet and shivering Voice, an exhausted and disheveled Harold, and an 18-year-old with a bag of Christmas presents to himself all board. Others are pushing and shoving to get onto the boat in time. A few injured islanders collapse as they step onto the boat. One of the guards by the dock says to the other, "Did the mayor mention anything about checking for a red 'A'?" The second guard looks at the first in disbelief. "I've seen enough ugly asses to last a lifetime. That's one order I quit following."

As one islander enters the boat, he throws up his hands and in a southern accent exclaims: "Free at last! Free at last! Almighty God, free at last!" The islander behind him turns around, "Free? Did you say we're free? Yeehaw!" The news passes through the line like wildfire, and a chorus of cheers echoes across the island. As the last of the islanders board, the first guard turns to the other, "Was that a dog that just got on?" The other guard stares at the first guard as if he is crazy. As the guards check their watches, they hurry onto the boat and signal the crew to set sail. As the islanders settle in the boat, they are filled with anticipation. Thoughts are now focused on what they will do once they are back.

With a last blast of the horn, the boat pulls away from the dock. The silhouette of the island looks rather harsh and unfamiliar as it becomes smaller. Was this their home for the past several months? The ride is smooth; almost too smooth.

Goldie immediately goes to the upper deck. But his glazed eyes are fixed on the bay, looking toward San Francisco, transfixed into another world. The tears are still frozen on his cheeks. Then he turns toward Alcatraz. Again, rushing footsteps, silence, and then a splash. The priest, now noticing what has happened, runs toward the end of the boat yelling "Goldie!" He continues yelling, "Stop the boat. Stop the boat! Man overboard!" He feels the boat accelerating as it moves farther from the dock. Turning around for help, he scans the crowd. "Somebody get the captain to stop this boat!" Some look away, and some look directly at him with eyes as cold as the water around Alcatraz. But no one takes a step. In amazement, the priest yells, "C'mon, haven't you learned anything?" He quickly turns around, struggling for a better look as he feels the railing loosening.

Should he jump in to save him? He puts one foot over the railing. Suddenly, a large fist grabs the back of his coat and pulls him back in the boat. He turns to hear a booming voice.

"No, Father," Harold firmly says.

"I can't find a life preserver," another voice screams.

A few rush to the captain's cabin, where their pleas fall on deaf ears.

"Turn back!"

"Open up!"

"Don't you care if he lives or dies?"

But the captain continues looking straight ahead toward the shore of San Francisco.

The priest looks out toward the ocean and sobs, "I lost sight of him."

"We'll send help when we reach the city," Harold replies. He accompanies the priest to a bench. With their heads bowed, the passengers on the outside deck look as if they are in prayer. Silence.

As they approach Pier 33, the silence remains. Most of the future city dwellers' eyes are now fixed on the dock ahead. Uneasiness.

As the boat docks, everyone is herded off. A caravan of buses awaits.

Now a bullhorn interrupts, "In a bus, everyone in a bus."

As Tricia takes a step into the first bus, she leans forward to ask, "Can't I just call a cab?"

The stone-faced driver responds, "Orders are 'everyone on the bus.'"

A passenger behind her yells, "Let's move it, honey!"

As the first bus is filled, the conversations pick up.

"What a' ya gonna do when you get back?" one of the passengers asks as the bus begins to jerk forward.

"Call my family. I'll probably break down crying," she responds with tears in her eyes.

The priest is running his hands through his hair, still in disbelief over the day's events. His thoughts focus on Goldie. Did he make it to shore? Is he alive? He now clasps his hands in prayer and whispers, "Oh, God, please help Goldie." The priest's clasp tightens as he prays for the injured, and the man that lost his life in the riot. Did he fulfill his purpose on the island? He hopes so, and hopes he had a positive impact on some lives. Where will God need him next? Will his congregation still need him? He does not worry, as he knows it is in God's hands.

A few seats in back of the priest is Harold, who is gazing out the window, focusing on nothing. He is in deep thought, as he ponders what life will be like when he returns. What will he say to his son? How has Donny changed in the last several months? If he learned anything during his stay at Alcatraz, it is that he misses his son more than he thought was possible. He wonders who has been coaching Donny's basketball team while he's been gone. He hopes there is an opening for a coach on his son's baseball team this upcoming season. One thing is for sure, he will give his son the biggest hug of his life. But when he walks through that door, his wife better not be there . . .

In the very back of the bus, the 18-year-old is bobbing his head up and down, listening to music from the earphones of a DigMe player confiscated from Richie's room. "Uh uh uh, badoo boom boom, deedee uh uh." He bends over and grabs a bottle labeled 'Cabernet Bleutet.' Without a corkscrew, he takes a screwdriver from his utility belt and plunges it into the cork of the bottle. Yanking it out, he tosses the cork behind him and takes a swig. He continues, "uh uh uh, badoo boom boom . . ."

Tricia is at the front of the bus scanning the scenery out the window. The waterfront area, which she used to pass in oblivion every day to work, suddenly becomes a freshly painted canvas. From Alcatraz it was just a smattering of dots, but now the downtown buildings seem to come alive. With Nan's reference, she should surely be able to land a top job downtown. Her vast knowledge of the city will serve her well. She takes in the downtown landmarks, and the familiar billboards, shops, and streets bring a comfort to her. They just pass Bush Street, so Mission Street should be coming up very soon. They'll be transported back to their holding cells, and then released. As she sees the sign for Mission Street approaching, she gently smiles. The bus should be turning any second now.

Her head makes the turn but the bus does not. She does a double take. Yes, she is not mistaken, that was Mission Street. Were they being transported to a different part of the city? Her heart suddenly picks up the pace. The bus now turns onto the freeway. Her heart now leaps out of her chest.

She stands up and yells, "I-80! I-80! Why are we taking I-80?"

Others now look out their windows.

"Hey, you missed the turn!"

"Where the hell are we goin'?"

The guard with metallic glasses, who has been standing at

the front of the bus, says with a grin and a New York accent, "New Yoke City."

There is an unbelieving silence followed by screaming, which causes the 18-year-old to drop his vintage bottle of wine, shattering it in a hundred pieces.

A man stands up and shouts in horror, "MURDER IS LEGAL IN NEW YORK!!!!"

Harold immediately puts his fist through the bus window, and yells while he runs at the guard, "Turn this fucking bus around!"

The guard points his rifle at Harold and yells back, "Sit down, asshole!" which stops Harold in his tracks. "I was given orders to fire if there's rioting. Now sit your asses down." He continues as he holds his gun in the air, "You see, my friends, there a two kinds of people in this world. Those with guns, and those without guns. Sit down and shut up."

Voice screams "You know what you are, just a dirty son-of-a- . . ." A barking sound accompanies his scream.

He is interrupted by a passenger cupping his hands and letting out an Eastwoodesque "Aahhhh, wahhh, wahhh wahhh."

Back in New York City, there are guards waiting at the bus depot. One of the guards jokes with the others. "Why are they shipping these homos here? If anything, they should ship 'em to Greenwich Village where all the other homos are."

"Why don't you pull out all the stops when you welcome those faggots? You could dress in your wife's clothes just like you always wanted," the other guard giggles.

"Screw you."

Bouquet

Goldie walks once again through the cellhouse on this fog drenched morning. He searches through each bar covered window for a sign of the sun.

"Doesn't matter," he thinks. His heart races as it always does as he approaches Rhonna's condo. She will most likely smile once again when he presents her with a flowering bouquet that only the gardens of Alcatraz can offer. Violets, blues, reds . . . the colors of the rainbow.

He lives for that smile. What *wouldn't* he do to see it?

As he passes each cell he recalls each and every time they walked together, there and back, to and from, his and her condo . . . just talking.

This morning though, his heart races a bit faster, his memories seem more vivid. It is as if past and present became one and the same. This makes him smile longer. He begins to run, he just can't wait . . . it is an anniversary . . . how long?

He runs as his thoughts race along with him. If they were all still here, surely they would congratulate him . . . cheer him on as he gets closer to Rhonna's unit. Flower petals from the bouquet shower the dim cellblock as they dance behind him, too weak for the journey, too slow for the race. Violets . . . Blues . . .

Suddenly he stops. He arrives with a knock on her door. No answer. Still a smile and the door opens.

"These are for you Rhonna . . . it is a special day! His arm reaches out with a bouquet dressed in morning dew. You can keep these with the others!"

As he steps inside, he notices the walls are covered with what appears to be graffiti. Writing, words in verse, paragraphs, some large, some small, he walks in . . . looks around . . . all covered; all of the walls, some with bold black writing, some with a soft blue, some with coal, some with blood.

"Is this from the riot?" Goldie asks in disbelief. "Who would do something like this?" As he approaches the wall, he attempts to read the handwriting.

Throw a chair through a rock
And a mask through a window
one in a thousand
Times I stared
through a mirror
A diamond mirror

Bewildered, he turns to the opposite wall and begins to read the next passage.

You left me a mark in time
A message with no words . . .

He moves closer to the wall, and his finger follows the sweeping verses. Verse upon verse, his motion becomes freer.

Not held together by crossbeams
or fixed on any foundation
Its strings too delicate to hold any relationships
or weather any storm.

A smile comes across Goldie's face. He closes his eyes, and reads the next verse aloud.

Love and Life
once held together by the same forces
have been razed forever.

He kneels down, but his hands are not in a prayer position. They are spread across the verses on the wall, and his eyes remain closed. His fingers scratch the wall in an attempt to feel the texture of the words. The words are repeated, but very slowly.

Love and Life
have been razed forever.

His head bows down as he repeats the same phrase quietly, even more slowly.

Love and Life
have been razed forever.

Ansell Roberts

As he opens his eyes, he raises his head and turns to see every bouquet he ever brought to her, carefully placed around the room as if in a funeral home; though every flower, in every color, is now dried and faded to muted tones of brown and rust.

His eyes search for Rhonna; past every flower, through every word written on every wall; around the room and back again.

But there is no one there.

Wedding Day

Goldie runs his hands through his hair. It's never been that long. His nails scratched at his thoughts. He sets a plate on one end of the wooden table, and in the fresh air waves a Western gull away. He steps around to the opposite side, to set another plate. As he sits down, he stares across the table. His eyes, with a starving blackness, gaze out over the iron railing and across the bay. Without moving them downward, with what is now almost a reflex, he brings his meal closer.

"Would you like a glass of the spirits with your meal, dear? Ah, thought so." His eyes move down toward his glass. "Tonight we'll walk the Agave Trail, and afterwards, well . . ."

As Goldie finishes his dinner, he slowly heads to where the agave plants grow. As he looks left, he says, "Remember the first time we walked down the trail? You had so much on your mind that night. I remember how we stumbled over a log right about there." He points to his right, then stops. "Here, let me hold your hand. It's getting dark." As he continues down the trail, he looks back and says, "Your hand is so warm." He then stops in his tracks and jerks his head back. "Did you hear that?" He backs up. Still not seeing anything, he whispers, "Stay right here; I'll be right back," as he takes the trail in a cautious gait.

His pace slows and he suddenly stops again . . . just to listen. People . . . the murmur of a crowd. His eyes squint down the path and focus near the old Barracks. He begins to move toward the small white structure nearby. The small chapel grows larger. Yes, it is the Church. It is time.

Goldie sees a crowd gathered in front of the stairs, leading up to the large wooden doors. The voices become louder. He now hears the individuals converse. "Where is she? How could this happen?" Familiar faces appear. A face with a smile of disbelief . . . another with a sneer. One glances at the flower girl and walks toward the street, shaking his head.

Goldie now walks to the top of the stairs. He ignores all of the voices, all of the faces, all except for one.

A silhouette of a young man is pacing back and forth at the door.

"Where is she? Where is she?"

The young man looks at his watch, and shakes his head.

Goldie's lips are in synch with the young man, echoing every word the young man says.

"She should have been here thirty minutes ago."

A light shines out as the door opens, with the chaplain emerging.

"Alex, maybe something unexpected came up. We could wait another half-hour if you like."

The young man whispers to himself, "Where is she?"

"Should I tell the guests to wait?"

"No. No, she would have been here by now. Tell them to go."

As the chaplain opens the door to go back in, the figure walks in the direction of Goldie.

Goldie asks, "Where is she?" Suddenly Goldie runs down the stairs and looks back to the Agave Trail, repeating, "Where is she?" His face becomes a mask of fear. His body tingles with loneliness, and a rapid heartbeat becomes a voice of silence.

No one is there.

Goldie turns his head in the direction of the figure, but it no longer exists. There is nothing but darkness, except for the beam from the lighthouse which circles the water.

The End

Cutting Room Floor ("Outtakes")

"There's so many A-holes, maybe it would've made more sense if the law just shipped the people who aren't A-holes to Alcatraz."

The viewer is so upset, she hits the viewer next to her. "How the hell can he get away with this!" She presses the offense button twice, which increments his total offenses from one to three. She hits the red "A" button so hard, it flies off the terminal onto the hot dog which the man with the sunglasses is biting into. Unknowingly, he swallows the red "A" button.

"That reminds me of when the United States was sealed off from foreigners."

The spring air around Alcatraz carries with it the moistness from the ocean breeze. The fog thickens as each morning goes by. With the fog, the island appears isolated, almost on a separate planet.

Early one morning, a foghorn goes off in a unique tune: Whooo, Whoooooo, Whoo, Whooo, WhOOOOO, Whoo, . . . A pause, and it goes off again. Then again, and again, incessantly for several minutes. This rude introduction to the morning awakens most islanders and causes some to bolt out of their rooms in anger.

"Let's find out who's doin' this and string him up the light tower!"

The horns are blaring even louder. Far behind this unfazed driver, amidst the smoke of overheated cars, a motorist is seen struggling to climb to the roof of his SUV. He sees the countless vehicles ahead, but not the cause... he takes off running. Jumping from one rooftop to the other ahead, trying to get closer to the story. One dent after the next, he finally sees the cause of this jam. "Hey, you motha, get into the van or I'll throw you into the bay!" He screams to no avail, the horns are louder than he can scream. Just as he is ready to advance, the car beneath him lurches ahead and he falls mercilessly backwards onto a hood ornament with a six inch wing span. This scream rises above the horns.

Richie takes in a reporter using VR—reporter let into Traz using VR. People see themselves on program and wonder how they get film of them. When they bust in his room, islanders put on VR and realize he exploited them. Richie wears sunglasses that are like camcorders. They film islanders and the images are transmitted to reporters back in the states. Common technology but economically out of reach—VR part of everday language—Richie has state of art stuff—businesses use it. "Eye on Traz"—cheeseball news program. Read his software—"Tahitian women with mangos", "Amazon woman in the rainforest". They pan through it. "This guy ain't locked up on an island—he's going everywhere! We're stuck in this hellhole and he's dancing with Tahitian women with mangos."

Strikers dress like regular people—anywhere at any time —like plain-clothes cop—maybe armpatch is only thing that describes them—little striker patch on arm.

Rhonna was caught wearing a sexy halter top in a cardiac unit of a hospital. Also at a party she spiked the jello with Everclear. People did not know and were getting drunk on jello cubes. Person on medication had a few cubes and then had a reaction. After finding out what she did the person reported her.

But a smile comes across her face as she remembers an incident she was not reported for. She was speeding when suddenly she screeched to a halt at a stop light. The man in the car alongside her at the stoplight turned his head in surprise as he saw the car hopping. As her window rolls down she gestures with her hand for him to come closer. As he rolls down his window, she says "I want to tell you a secret." His head pops out of the car window, and when this happens she takes out a huge police-horn and shouts on the top of her lungs, and the loud sound from the speakers cause his hair to stand on end. She then laughs as she pulls away. The man screams as he holds both of his ears. She thought to herself that he probably couldn't call to report her because he couldn't hear anything. Suddenly her thoughts are interrupted by Goldie.

The 18-year-old can relate stories of how he called the viewers on a few occasions to report A-hole—but when they reviewed the tape they realized he was the A-hole.

One incident was when he wouldn't let a car pass him up—when they sped up to pass him he sped up—The other car barely cut in front of him just in time to avoid an accident (almost hit an oncoming car)—he wound up swerving into a ditch. The oncoming car also swerved into the ditch.

"That's the sign of a true social degenerate—it would never occur to them that they are one. They never think that they hurt anyone."

He puts his arm around her waist as he embraces her. Their lips meet, and this night will not outlast their embrace.

On their subsequent walks, they are closer, often joining hands.

Spring-Summer,

Goldie-Rhonna,

Fall-Winter

"I don't think it's possible to make him a bigger asshole than he already is (after placing firecracker on his seat cushion)."

Goldie and Rhonna have lost track of time, as have many islanders. No watches, clocks, or calendars to dictate time. Just nature's rhythms. The sun, bursting through the iron bars on each outside window frame, casts shadows along the corridors of the cell house. The length and angle of these sundial-striped shadows reveal the time of day to the islanders.

Outside the cell house, the islanders have learned to "read" the trajectory of the sun for the time of day, letting them know mealtime or task time. The fog on many summer days leaves the islanders guessing, however.

What the heck was that?
What?
That sound . . . it sounded like a giant . . .
What the? Look over there!
Holy . . . the bridge. The whole damn bridge is . . .
I can't look.

Near the San Francisco bay, one teenager is looking through a telescope at Alcatraz. His older friend tells him "We're wasting our time here. Why would anyone be left on Alcatraz?" The younger teenager responds "Maybe someone got left behind when the boat left—or maybe someone is looking for some remnants." The older friend laughs "Well, if there's a telescope powerful enough to see it, it's yours." The younger friend prods him to look through the telescope, which he does. The older friend says "I do see a shadow on the big hill—it looks like a shadow of someone." The younger friend pushes the older one out of the way as he peeps through the scope. "You're right, it has a gown and gavel—it looks like a shadow of a judge. You think a judge is on the island?" The older one peeps through the scope and adds "Yeah, what else can it be?"

The two gaze a bit more. They are surprised to see the shadow moving. "You think anyone will believe us?" the younger one asks. "Nope, not a one. You're better off citing the Loch Ness monster," the older one responds. After an hour or so the two leave with the telescope. Alcatraz was quiet that night, except for the wind and waves crashing at the shore— and a constant pounding as if from a gavel.

Back at the control room. "Did you feel someth . . . there it is again. Oh geez . . ."
"A quake. A . . ."

Few kegs left as islanders drink and have their "own" therapy sessions—much more productive.

"Look at the size of my fuckin' glasses! And I still can't see a thing." As he says this in a mock drunken voice, he turns away from the Cubs-Giants game on his computer screen and asks his co-worker "Is it breaktime?"
His co-worker is staring at the screen "Wipe off those goggles and check out this blonde, Harry."
The first man continues in his mock voice "By the way, who's playing this game?"
As the second man laughs, he says to the first "Hey, enough of this, let's take a break."
The first man continues, "All right, let me hear ya'. A 1, a 2, a take me out to . . ."
As both men head out the door. . .

Goldie watches as the figure runs down toward the waiting limousine. The young man takes the ring out of his pocket and throws it into the open window. He runs past the automobiles in the procession, past the streamers, the balloons, and the white houses down the block. Goldie watches him run until there is no sign of him.

One day all three 'volunteers' are taking the clean laundry out of the numerous dryers and putting them in their appropriate bags that are tagged.

Goldie says as he picks up a bundle of laundry containing a very large bras:

"Whoa man, who's packing this?"

His overweight, balding co-worker responds, "What room is the bag tagged for?"

"Let's see, unit 44."

"Oh, yeah, that's Jeri Anderson. She used to be a penthouse model. I talked to her on the way over hear—she sounded very lonely."

"Are you pullin' my leg—a penthouse model? And lonely?"

"Not at all. You'll see when she picks up her laundry."

"I think I'll deliver this laundry to her personally. Wouldn't want her to pick up a bag with such a heavy bras. She may rupture herself.

"I know her condo has many flowers in it—especially roses."

"I could get her a few roses from the flowerbed. That may be a nice way to introduce myself."

The woman in the laundry room is a little farther away, but

appears to be listening to the conversation but not saying anything. She spits a wad of tobacco a few feet away from the laundry.

Goldie is decked out in full regalia, hair slicked back, with clean laundry in one hand and roses in the other as he rings the doorbell of unit 44. A voice from the unit indicates she'll be right there. As the door opens, a very plump woman in her 50's opens the door. Goldie's face turns ghost white, and the flowers fall from his hands.

The following day, Richie is seen by Tricia, who is passing by him on Broadway.

"What time you got?"

Richie stops to check his wristwatch. "1:50" he replies, then continues to walk. He abruptly stops, reaches in his sportcoat pocket, and checks his blackberry. He looks straight ahead, and turns sharply back toward his condo. His pace begins to hurry, then suddenly slows as he enters his condo.

Tricia continues walking, and sharply turns the corner to the next aisle. But as the islander is ready to step in the next aisle, she suddenly overhears a disgruntled voice.

"So now I know who you went to Lahaina with."

"What are you talking about?"

"Where were you last Friday and Saturday?"

"What?"

"Don't give me this. I saw you talkin' outside his condo last week."

"What in the hell are you talking about?"

"Richie. You even sat with him in the dining hall last week."

As Rhonna returns a look of disbelief, Goldie continues "His room. Rumor is you've been in his room."

As she continues with an intense look of disbelief, Goldie's voice heightens "I know all about it—wet-bar, cherry cabinet, a virtual reality set out of this world. All for a nice price tag—a beautiful brunette."

Rhonna shakes her head and screams, "Ugggh", as she runs to her condo with arms flapping.

As she disappears in her room, Goldie yells, "You threw it all away, babe."

Tricia, who has been listening at the corner of the aisle all along, now quickly retraces her footsteps.

Meanwhile, a few of the new islanders step into what appears to be a decrepid building on the western shore of the island. A mesh of steel bars in place of window panes covers both stories of this building like large stripes. "Are our condos in here?" a voice says in disbelief. "What are these machines?" a voice asks in shock. The shadows from these antiquated machines and steel bars violently collide. "It looks like metal shop machines from a century ago. Let's get out of here, the air stinks." A few are coughing as they head outside.

"Crap! What if the Cubs win the World Series?"